NOT QUITE
A BARONESS

THE BOSTON HEIRESSES BOOK 2

AVA ROSE

CONTENTS

ISBN-13: 978-0-6484045-3-8

First Edition
Published by Jen Katemi (Flourish Books)

CHAPTER ONE

ARMSTRONG-LEEDS HOUSE, BOSTON

October 1891

Her Royal Highness, Princess Elizabeth Armstrong-Leeds, Baroness Esk, had been through enough ordeal for a lifetime. Getting kidnapped by a man who had posed as a pen friend and admirer, and then being held in a dungeon and forced to sign marriage papers, had taken a toll. Any lady with a constitution weaker than Libby's would have crumbled under it all.

But here she was in the drawing room of her home with her best friend, Lady Anna Trevallyn, going through the latest fashion magazines in search of the perfect wedding dress style for Anna. The best part of it all was that Anna was getting married to Libby's brother Penforth. A match Libby had been hoping for, for a long time.

"What about this one?" Her younger sister Mary joined in the discussion, poking her brown head between them from behind the sofa. "I do love the lace frills."

Libby stared at the dress in question and shook her head, just as a snort from Anna confirmed it. The two shared a quick smile. Despite the fact that Anna was a duchess, lace and frills were not her style. "Definitely not."

"But a wedding dress should have a lot of lace," Mary argued.

"Will you two darlings allow Anna to make her own choice?" Libby's mother Christiana was seated on the other sofa, reading the day's papers.

"Is there anything interesting in the paper today, Mama?" Libby asked.

Her mother, understanding her meaning perfectly, raised a brow. "What does it say about *you*, you mean?"

The papers had already had a thing or two to say about Libby's scandal, on a daily basis, it seemed, and although her mother and Anna always discouraged her from reading, Libby's curiosity was stronger than their warnings. What she read pained her, of course, but she learned from it. Society could be cruel, especially to an unwed lady who had brought scandal to her name. Libby felt it would be easier to bear if she took the meted punishment alone, but Boston society did not work that way. Instead, her entire family had to be dragged through the dirt along with her.

"It doesn't say anything," her mother announced with a sudden smile.

Libby moved to sit beside her mother and took the paper, flipping the pages and anticipating libel. She found nothing. Her mother had spoken the truth.

"I don't understand," she said. "Not that I'm complaining, but…*why?*"

Anna piped up. "It means those vultures of the press have finally lost interest in your situation."

Dare she hope? Dare she hope that at last, there was some respite from it all?

"Have you ever known *The Brahmin Times* to carry a story for more than two weeks?" Anna asked.

It was true. Scandals happened all the time and a fresher story was sure to take the place of hers. She turned the pages and found it. The new story.

The engagement of Lady Dianne Belleville to Lord Remington, a prominent political figure.

Libby released a sigh of relief. She had spent the past two weeks—since the time of her rescue—on tenterhooks. She could not go out and did not receive callers. But now, at last, she was free. Perhaps she could finally—

"My lady," called Antoine, their butler.

All four ladies turned their heads expectantly in his direction.

"Lady Elizabeth," the butler clarified.

"Yes?" Libby asked.

"Mr. Graves from the Boston Police Department requests a word with you, my lady." Antoine's nose wrinkled, as if the visitor had brought in a bad smell.

"He's here?" Mr. Graves had been in charge of her kidnapping case. His presence in her home today suggested two things. One: Sir Anthony, her kidnapper, had possibly been caught. Unfortunately, he had gotten away when his accomplices had been arrested. Two: the police needed more information from her. They seemed to be requesting a lot of that, lately.

With a sigh, she got to her feet. "Where is he?"

"Still in the foyer, my lady."

"Show him to the small salon. I shall join him

shortly." She smoothed her hands over the skirt of her jade green and cream dress and straightened her shoulders.

"Do you want me to come with you?" Anna offered. She seemed to understand exactly how Libby felt every time the police turned up. Anna had been through a lot, too. No doubt she disliked reliving the torment as much as Libby did.

Libby nodded, grateful for her friend's continued support, and together they walked out of the drawing room and across the grand foyer where they met Pen. Her brother must have been informed of Mr. Graves' presence also, because he was headed toward the salon.

Mr. Graves was standing when they entered. He had come alone, thankfully. He often arrived accompanied by another officer or two, their presence only adding to her aggravation. None of them took a seat.

"Has he been found?" Pen asked without so much as a greeting.

The expression on Mr. Graves' face was rather queer and it stirred a feeling of anxiousness within Libby. There was something terrible going on.

"A *body* has been found," the policeman answered in a slow drawl.

Oh, no! The blood drained away from her face

and she felt suddenly a little dizzy. Beside her, she heard Anna's sharp intake of breath and then felt her friend reach out and squeeze Libby's hand. She felt numb, unable to squeeze back.

"Yesterday, we found a body in a ditch just outside of Boston. It was identified to be a Mr. Nolan Hart."

She did not recognize the name Nolan. Perhaps it was not as she had feared. Perhaps this Nolan was a relative of Sir Anthony's, or another of his victims, a very unfortunate one.

Pen frowned and took a step forward. "Nolan?"

"Yes," Graves replied. "Mr. Nolan Anthony Hart."

It was him! The last criminal had been captured, but not alive. Libby's thoughts tumbled. Was she sorry that he was dead? She was not certain. On the one hand, she felt it was deserved given what he had put her through. On the other, she didn't *want* to be glad that someone was dead.

"How did he die?" Pen asked. He was doing all of the talking, for which she was grateful. She wasn't sure her voice would work, right now.

"Multiple stab wounds to the body, and trauma to the head," Mr. Graves replied.

Libby slowed her breathing, trying to banish the image his words had just conjured.

Stay calm, she told herself. *Stay calm*.

"He was murdered, then." Pen stated the obvious.

"Indeed." Graves nodded before turning to Libby and pulling out a small book and a pen. "I would like to ask you a few questions, Lady Elizabeth, if you don't mind."

Why did that statement suddenly make her feel even more drained and anxious?

"Go on," she said, as calmly as she could.

"Records show that you are married to this man. What can you confirm about this marriage?"

She scoffed inwardly at the term. It was hardly a marriage when her captor had drugged her and then threatened to harm Mary if she refused. "It was a forced marriage. I was kidnapped, imprisoned and my family threatened. I thought I had no choice," she said carefully. The memory constricted her already aching chest.

"Pardon the crassness of my next question. Has this marriage been…err…consummated in any way?" The officer's eyes were intent when he asked the question. He was clearly trying to discern her reaction.

Her cheeks heated uncomfortably. "No, it has not." *Thankfully*. She didn't know what she would have done if that had happened. "I was held captive throughout until my rescue from that crypt under the church." Captive beneath a chapel where she'd had to share the silence with the dead while the fear of never being found ate away at her will to fight. Her whole body began to tremble at the memory.

Graves' gaze then turned to Penforth, and for the first time, she saw her brother look concerned. "Is there any action being taken against this marriage?"

Pen answered firmly. "Yes, an annulment has already been filed."

Graves nodded as he finished scrawling in the book and put it away in his coat before addressing Libby again. "Princess Elizabeth Armstrong-Leeds, Baroness Esk, I regret to inform you that you are the primary suspect in the murder of your husband, Mr. Nolan Anthony Hart."

Very slowly, all feeling and perception drained from her, leaving only numbness. Somehow, her mind had known this was coming, and yet, now that the policeman had uttered the words, she felt as though her spirit had left her body and was observing the scene from a distance.

"We will need to take you into custody as we further investigate," the officer announced.

Libby couldn't think. She felt Anna's arm snake

around her waist as Pen released a loud curse. "That's preposterous! Do you know who she is?" Her brother spoke in a low, menacing tone and he stepped close to stand beside her and Anna.

"Sir—"

"Lady Elizabeth is royalty, and a baroness in her own right, and one of the most prominent members of Boston's elite. You seriously expect you will be allowed to simply take her into custody?"

The officer's mouth opened and closed a couple of times. He was obviously contemplating the wisdom of crossing her brother.

"Go on," Pen said. The tone was dangerous now. "Take her."

Mr. Graves shook his head. "I…I…th-think she can remain here while we…investigate."

"Good choice. Now get out there and do your job. Find the real culprit." Pen's gaze was fierce as he added, "If I see you inside this house again, the police will have a real murder suspect to deal with."

The officer practically ran out of the room. What Pen had done was brave but also futile. It might have scared off Graves for today, but it would not keep the police away. Graves was only a low-ranking member of the department. His superiors were sure to follow up, and her brother would not be able to protect her forever.

Anna turned to her then, saying something. Libby saw her friend's mouth move, but she could not hear a word. Instead, her own shocked thoughts were screaming in her head, deafening her to all else. Her legs began to move as if of their own will, slowly carrying her across the room and out into the foyer. Her mother rushed up to her, grabbing her hand and talking to her. Again, she did not hear.

Christiana pulled Libby into her arms and she could feel hands running up and down her back in a consoling motion. The noise in her head only grew louder.

She dragged herself free of her mother's embrace and climbed the stairs in stiff, mechanical motions. When she reached her rooms, she let herself in and then turned the key in the lock. And that was when the chaotic noise in her head stopped, and everything she was supposed to be feeling finally let loose.

As if she had been hit, her legs gave way and she collapsed to the carpeted floor. Her hands went up to clutch her head and she curled her body into a ball.

She had thought she was ruined before. She was truly ruined now. And so was her family…especially Mary who was only sixteen and yet to make her entry into society.

With a sister kidnapped and forced into marriage, then suspected of the murder of her kidnapper husband, there was no hope of Mary joining respectable society, much less finding a suitor. *She will be ostracized, and all because of me.*

Libby was a free spirit and, for herself, could not care less what society made of her. Whatever worry ate at her, was for her family. Her ruination did nothing to change her own plans, for she'd never quite fancied marriage. Unless the man was extraordinary. Anthony Hart, much to her regret, had almost made her fall for him in the lovely letters he had sent over the months of their correspondence, but after what had transpired, she didn't think she could ever trust again.

She had never met him prior to the incident, and she had first received his letter several months ago. The man had written that he had seen her at one of the balls she and Anna had attended but never got the chance to be introduced. Libby had felt a sense of adventure in corresponding with a man she had never met; it had been intriguing. The image he had presented was that of the perfect man, someone she could imagine herself with; an advocate for equality, intellectual and well-traveled. They had very similar interests and she could not help but be enchanted by him.

He had wanted to meet her in person and had said so many times. His last letter, which had arrived a month before her abduction, had contained an invitation to meet in Cambridge. At first, Libby had been incredibly happy and even penned down the location and date, but after some days and a bit more thinking, she felt that something was wrong with the invitation. Why would a gentleman ask a lady to meet with him for the first time outside of town, and without a chaperone? It did not make sense. It was not proper. So, she had declined his invitation. She had thought to invite him to the house instead but decided against that, too. In the end, she did not trust his motives.

One evening, during a soirée that she and Anna had been hosting at the latter's home, Libby had had a dress mishap and retired upstairs to change. On catching a light flashing repeatedly outside her bedchamber window, Libby had decided to go investigate, despite her mind's caution. That had been the moment she was taken.

If only I hadn't been so stupid that night. I should have listened to my inner voice.

There were many things that she did not remember. They had covered her nose with a cloth and everything had gone black. When her senses returned, she had been tied to a chair in a dark crypt, miserable and alone.

Her trust had been broken and her faith almost shattered, but Anna and Pen had saved her. Now, it appeared she was in another hell. They would not be able to get her out of it this time, for Sir Anthony—no, *Mister*—Hart was determined, even in death, to pull her down.

Libby's ability to marry or not, no longer mattered. She was done with it. But it did matter for Mary. Her younger sister should not be deprived of the right to wed, because of the actions of a selfish, callous man. It was not fair.

She dragged herself up from the floor and moved to the large four-poster bed. Pulling back the covers, she lay down and pulled them back up to her chin. I just need some rest, she thought. From her memories, and from the cruelty of life.

Libby closed her eyes and allowed her head to sink into the soft pillow. Her eyes stung, but she dared not let the tears fall. Once she did, she feared they might never stop. Instead, she took this moment of peace and drew from it. She would need all the strength she had, and then some, to find the will to fight this to the end.

CHAPTER TWO

ALGONQUIN CLUB, BOSTON

That evening

Detective Henry DeHavillend's ears worked like a predator's when he was in public places, especially in exclusive gentlemen's clubs. He picked up names, voices, even tones, from all around him. He was at his table now, leaning back in his chair and sipping the last of his whiskey.

Moments like this were usually an ideal way to relax after a long day of roaming the streets of Boston solving mysteries, but not for Henry. He only stopped working when he was asleep, and even then, he sometimes woke to pen down something he had thought, or rather dreamed about, while sleeping.

"Would you like another, my Lord?" A waiter hovered nearby.

Henry cast a lazy glance at his empty snifter before giving the man a curt nod. The glass was refilled quickly, and Henry left alone to once again indulge in listening and thinking. The Algonquin's service was beyond reproach.

Were Henry merely a detective, membership in one of the most exclusive clubs in Boston would have been well-nigh impossible, even given his reputation as one of the most ruthless private detectives in the state. When the police department was unable to solve a case, they called him in. Despite their numerous offers to lure him to work with them officially, he had remained adamant about staying independent. He worked best without meddling from others.

His reputation was not the reason he had secured membership in this club. That bonus had been a boon from his family. Henry was a Viscount, and the first son of the renowned DeHavillend family who held prestige and wealth both in England and the United States of America. His family had everyone courting their favor. Everyone, except Henry himself. He couldn't distance himself enough from the life he was supposed to enjoy now that the title had passed to him. He couldn't imagine anything less satisfying than embracing life as The Right Honorable, the Viscount Henry DeHavillend.

He'd eschewed a life of luxury in favor of a more exciting existence. A life where he was fulfilled, and where he had a purpose outside of carrying the family title. In fact, he had given up every advantage except membership in this fine establishment. It helped with his work and, to be honest, he enjoyed his time alone in the private sitting area that was always reserved for his use.

Tonight, he was working on a theft case. Lady Kingsleigh had woken to her necklace missing, and it was not just any necklace, either. The missing piece included a rare black diamond in its setting. This was not a hugely exciting case, and he had only taken it up as a favor to the family, but it served to occupy his time until something more interesting came along.

"DeHavillend, you devil!" The unmistakable stentorian voice of his friend, Samuel Mast, boomed from behind him.

He turned, the beginnings of a smile turning up the corners of his mouth. "Mast."

Samuel clapped him on the back before taking

the seat opposite him. "You won't believe what I heard today," he said. The man loved bringing Henry stories.

He relaxed in his chair. "What happened this time?"

"Remember that kidnapped princess—the one who's also a baroness? The Armstrong-Leeds girl everyone was talking about?" At Henry's nod, he leaned closer and lowered his voice. "Her kidnapper has been found dead in a ditch outside of town. He was murdered."

Henry's curiosity bubbled up. He tried to tamp it back down, but couldn't help the question that popped out. "Are there any suspects?"

"That is the most interesting part." Samuel's eyes darted from side to side, making sure no one was listening. "*She* is the suspect."

Henry nodded calmly. The man had purportedly kidnapped the woman and forced her to marry him under duress. In this society, that was death to a woman's reputation. *There* was a motive for murder.

Samuel frowned. "You don't look surprised."

"That is because I am not."

"But you have to admit that this is a curious case."

He shrugged. "On the contrary. It is rather

straightforward. Given what happened to the woman, I would suggest she is very much capable of such a crime."

Samuel's brows drew together. "She couldn't have carried it out herself, surely? That is to say, the girl is quite dainty."

"Well, she could easily have hired someone to do her dirty bidding."

"Ah, I see." His friend brightened. "That should make this case exciting, shouldn't it?"

Henry raised his glass, pausing to watch the play of light on the cut crystal before touching it to his lips. "Not to me."

That was a lie. This was just the sort of case he would ordinarily love to chase, but for some reason he wanted to stay out of this one if he could. He didn't want to be the one to prove a genteel lady's guilt. Not when she had clearly been through so much, already.

"You're saying you're not even going to consider taking it?" Samuel made a funny, begging face.

"No."

He sighed. "Oh, well."

"Is that all you have for me?" Henry asked.

Samuel grinned, undeterred by Henry's gruffness. "Perhaps some time with a friend, and a drink or two, is what brought me here."

Henry chuckled. "Why do you put up with me?"

"Honestly? Because you're interesting," his friend answered.

Henry called for a fresh round of drinks, and the two chatted for a while. After about an hour, Samuel left. Not long after his departure, Henry saw a tall, dark-haired man come into the room. After exchanging a few words with the steward of the establishment, he advanced into the room and headed rather obviously toward Henry.

He didn't need any introduction to recognize this man. His limping gait was as telling of his identity as if his name had been shouted out to the entire room. Henry shifted in his seat, feeling suddenly uncomfortable. He did not like this man very well. He was arrogant, entitled, and always in ill-humor. Henry greatly disliked the energy that surrounded the man. And at this moment, given the conversation he'd just had with Samuel, he especially did not want to start a conversation with the brother of the kidnapped Armstrong-Leeds woman.

"Lord DeHavillend," Sir Penforth drawled as he stopped before him.

"Your Royal Highness."

The man rolled his eyes. "Penforth, please."

Without asking, he lowered himself into the seat opposite.

"This is most improper," Henry said. He tried to keep his tone even despite his growing irritation. "Invading a man's privacy like this."

Sir Penforth shrugged. "I am not known for following the codes of propriety." He raised his hand and gestured for the waiter to serve him.

Henry's eyes narrowed as he regarded the gentleman in front of him. They'd had little cause to meet and in the few times they had—before Henry had embraced the life of mystery-solving—they had not taken to each other. Henry's attempts at congeniality had been met with a cold wall, and he had decided Sir Penforth was not the sort of man with whom he wished to spend time.

"To what do I owe this honor, Penforth?" He knew why the man was here, of course.

"I would like you to take up my sister's case."

Henry snorted and took a leisurely sip of his drink. "I don't take cases like that. I solve mysteries. I don't chase after kidnappers."

He was careful not to reveal any newly gained knowledge about the case.

"You will take this one," the prince drawled. "You want excitement, don't you?"

Henry's brows made a slow ascent toward his hairline.

"The man who took my sister has been found dead," Sir Penforth stated. "And Baroness Esk is a suspect."

Henry made a show of looking bored. "As I said, I don't take cases like this. But I am curious about one thing."

"Yes?"

"Why do you not refer to your sister by her higher title of princess?"

Sir Penforth's jaw clenched. "Not that it is any of your business, but it is her choice. She feels that the royal title is too...restrictive for her modern lifestyle. She prefers the other. Now, back to the matter at hand. Name your price, and I will double it."

"It is not about money," Henry responded tersely. He did not want to take this case, despite the fact that a small part of him was intrigued by a society woman who chose not to embrace the highest of titles. *Confound it.* He did not *want* this case. Why was everyone pushing it on him?

"What is it about, then?" This man was not going to let go.

With a weary sigh, Henry finally answered. "I am not taking it because I think she is guilty."

The response caused Sir Penforth's eyes to darken dangerously and Henry put up his hand, palm out. "Now, before you have me drawn and quartered, I am only being realistic. It does appear that the chances of your sister committing this crime are quite high given the ordeal she has been through. And *if* she is guilty, I do not want to be the one to prove that."

His explanation did nothing to put out the fire in the prince's eyes. If anything, his look was murderous now.

"I also do not want to be expected to cover it up if she is found guilty. I am in the business of exposing crimes, not covering them up."

"She is not guilty," Sir Penforth said through clenched teeth.

"She is your sister and you are certainly allowed to have faith in her. I am a detective and I do not know her at all."

The murderous glare disappeared from Sir Penforth's eyes as he let out a sigh. Henry experienced a moment of sympathy for the man. He had sisters too, and although he had not seen them in years, he cared deeply for them and would lay down his life for them if needed.

From a brother to a brother, he knew what Sir

Penforth must be going through. A lot of emotion. All the more reason to steer clear of this case.

"I am sorry," he said quietly and perhaps Sir Penforth could see he meant it, because he nodded solemnly before rising to his feet.

"If you ever change your mind, you know where to find me."

After he left, Henry sat for a very long time, thinking. As much as he suspected the princess's guilt, a tiny seed had been planted. *What if she is innocent?* He did not want to ignore the possibility of her innocence. His thoughts had him torn.

If she truly were innocent and he ignored her case, would the police be up to the task? In their incompetence, would they perhaps declare her guilty regardless of the truth? If that were to happen, it would be a travesty and he would not be able to forgive himself. *Damnation!* He needed more time to think.

He stood slowly, feeling tired, and retrieved his hat and greatcoat before making his way out of the club and into the night. The chill night air brushed his cheeks and he tilted up his head to allow the light rain to fall upon his face.

Unlike most people, he loved the rain and did not mind getting drenched. He walked down the street through the blanket of fog that had settled over the quieted city, making his way toward his apartment rooms in the diverse South End.

He only hired a carriage to take him home from the club when he had drunk too much, and that was a very rare occasion. Walking in the night was another of his odd likes. The darkness helped him think.

Henry didn't attend social functions unless he had to. He had little patience for such events and even less patience for the people who hosted and attended them. He did not mingle in the elite Boston Brahmin circle unless it was tied to a case on which he was working. And he had long moved out of his family's townhouse in Beacon Hill to a small suite of apartments in South End. But still, he knew of Her Royal Highness, Lady Elizabeth Armstrong-Leeds. Although they had not officially met, he knew her by reputation.

And not the reputation she had now, generated by recent events and adverse press. No, instead he had heard of her previously, in relation to her quest for equality. She had been known before her kidnapping as a fearless advocate for women, challenging any man who dared stand in her way. Life was quite remarkable in the way it dealt blows to certain people. Who would have thought a woman like Lady Elizabeth could be brought so low?

Perhaps he should take this case.

Henry could not explain why, but something was pulling him toward this case, despite every instinct against it. The feeling that he might regret it if he didn't take on the case, was becoming stronger than his need to stay away from the higher echelons of society.

CHAPTER THREE

ARMSTRONG-LEEDS HOUSE

The following day

 ibby had not slept a wink. Neither had she seen anyone nor eaten a bite since yesterday afternoon. Her door had remained locked since then, too. In the evening, her mother had knocked and called her name, asking if she was all right. She had responded briefly, to say she was fine and needed some space. A food tray had been left by the door which had remained untouched throughout the night. She suspected it had now been taken away.

With stiff shoulders, an even stiffer back and a leaden heart, she got out of bed, still in yesterday's dress, and moved toward the door where she unlocked it before ringing for her lady's maid, Grace. Then she crossed to the window to look out onto the busy street below.

Everyone carried on with their lives. Some were oblivious to her existence; some knew her but were unaware of her suffering; some liked her suffering; while others would commiserate.

But none of that mattered. She only wanted Mary to be received kindly by these people, and for Anna's reputation not to be tarnished given she was marrying into the family. She could help neither Mary nor Anna by sitting in her room wallowing in misery. It was time to stop the self-pity and start to make a plan.

A knock sounded. It was Grace, who entered with something like worry on her face. She curtsied and greeted Libby who nodded in return.

"Would you run me a bath and help me change out of this dress, please?"

As her corset was unlaced, her chest expanded as her lungs filled. Her ribs ached from being bound for so long. She took her time in the warm bath.

Three weeks ago, the only concern she'd had

was proving that she and Anna were fighting for the right cause. Now, the focus was on dragging her family out of this scandal. She had already taken responsibility for allowing herself to be beguiled and then kidnapped. She was not going to allow Penforth to take sole responsibility for mending things. That burden was hers.

WHEN SHE REACHED THE DINING ROOM, HER ENTIRE family was there. They all murmured greetings and although they tried to appear calm, she sensed their collective worry.

"Good morning," she said stiffly without looking at any one of them in particular. A footman pulled out a chair for her.

After her cup had been filled with coffee and she had added cream and sugar, she looked up to find everyone staring at her.

"I don't want concern over me to take away your appetites," she said. "Please eat."

"Darling," Christiana began, "are you all right?"

How could she be? She nodded. "I am fine, Mama."

"Are you sure?"

She nodded again and looked directly into her

mother's eyes. "I didn't do it and that is enough. I'm not going anywhere."

Coffee was all she was able to take. The feeling of unease in her stomach would not settle.

Anna reached across the table and squeezed her hand, and beside her, Pen took her other hand. "We're here," he said.

"I know. Thank you." The tears threatened to spill just then, but she fought them and they stayed put. She would not let them see her cry. It would just worry them more.

"Sir," came Antoine's voice from the doorway. A very welcome distraction.

"Yes?" Pen answered.

"Detective DeHavillend is here to see you."

Libby's shoulders slumped. *Another police officer?* Pen could not protect her forever. But then something about Pen caught her attention. He seemed pleased. And the name registered with her.

"DeHavillend? The Viscount, who dabbles in detecting?" She caught Pen's coat sleeve when he nodded. "Did you call him?"

"Yes," he replied.

Libby released him. DeHavillend had a reputation for being a great private detective. No case he'd ever taken up had remained unsolved.

Perhaps he could help prove her innocence and end her current plight.

She shot to her feet.

HENRY'S FIRST ORDER OF THE DAY WAS TO CALL ON the Armstrong-Leeds House and accept Sir Penforth's offer. As he alighted from the carriage, he looked up at the grand house that reminded him of his own family's home and prayed he was doing the right thing.

When he had woken this morning, he had decided he would only see this case to a conclusion if he was convinced of the princess's innocence. He would make that clear to Sir Penforth.

A stiff-backed, gray-haired butler with a downturned mouth answered his knock and looked him over from the top of his head to the toes of his shoes before clearing his throat and asking, "May I help you?"

"I am Detective DeHavillend. Sir Penforth is expecting me."

The starchy butler raised a skeptical brow. "He has not informed me."

Henry shrugged. "That is not my problem."

"Wait here, please."

Henry quipped, "I am not going anywhere."

The butler closed the door and after some minutes—Henry was not counting—he reappeared and asked Henry to enter. He was led to an opulent salon decorated in shades of dark green and brown where Sir Penforth waited.

"DeHavillend," he greeted. "I take it you are interested in helping me."

"Yes, but conditionally."

Sir Penforth's eyes narrowed. "State your condition."

"I will only see this case through if she is innocent."

"She *is* innocent," he affirmed.

"I will determine that."

One corner of Sir Penforth's mouth tilted up. "You will see this case through, I promise you."

His faith in his sister was rather admirable.

"May I see her?" Henry asked.

No sooner had the question come out of his mouth than a voice behind him uttered, "I am already here."

He turned around and his thoughts deserted him right then. All he had ever seen of the baroness were pictures and drawings, and she looked much different in the flesh. She was very fetching despite the remnants of bruising around her left eye, her jaw, and her right cheek. Eyes of hazel, almost amber, looked expectantly at him; and soft full lips of pink parted to speak.

"I am Lady Elizabeth."

Oh, he didn't need to be told that. For some unaccountable reason, his heart sped up.

"My lady," he bowed in a courtly manner. She remained standing which incited him to ask, "Are you going to sit?"

She shook her dark head. "I prefer to stand."

"I have a lot of questions for you—"

"So do I," she inserted.

She had questions for *him*? Henry was not easily surprised, but she had managed it.

"Oh? Then perhaps you *should* sit. We are going to be here for quite some time."

"Very well." She moved gracefully across the space and took a seat, folding her hands primly on her lap and tilting her head.

Her brother took a seat as well and finally, Henry did the same.

"Shall we?" he began. At her nod of approval, he said, "I am going to ask you questions you have no doubt been asked many times before, so bear with me."

Her expression softened at his words, reminding Henry he had to be gentle and treat her not as a criminal but as a person. A person with feelings.

"How were you taken?"

She lowered her eyes to her hands on her lap as she spoke. "I was staying with my friend Anna at Wrexford House. We were hosting a soirée and I had a dress mishap and went upstairs to my room to change. There was a strange light flashing outside my window in the garden and I went to check it out."

"You are very brave to go outside alone to check a mysterious light at night."

"It was not brave," she said quietly. "It was stupid." He could hear the self-reproach in her tone.

"What happened then?"

"I went out via the entrance near the servants' quarters, to avoid the guests. Someone grabbed me on my way out before I could reach the garden."

"I see." He narrowed his eyes, trying to ascertain her veracity.

"You're not going to take notes?" There was sarcasm in her tone.

He smiled blandly. "I am not one of those police officers who have been pestering you."

"Clearly."

"How much time did you spend conscious?"

One of her delicately winged brows rose and she gave him an 'are you seriously asking me that' look. "I did not have a watch, my Lord."

Henry swallowed back a smile. He had expected her to say that she did not know; instead, she had a witty rejoinder. "I prefer Detective rather than my Lord, if you please."

"Are you not a Viscount?" Her brows descended.

"I am, but I prefer not to use the title."

"Very well."

"Were you physically harmed while you were with your captors?"

The amber flecks in her eyes sparked with what he could only assume to be contained rage, and her entire body stiffened. He had been asking the right questions to gauge her emotions and this question hit right where he wanted it.

"Look at my face, Detective," was all she said.

He frowned. "Which one of them hit you?"

"Mr. Hart, and the chapel minister."

"And now a delicate question." He hesitated, then asked what had to be asked. "Your marriage. Has anything occurred to solidify it?"

"Definitely not. My brother has filed for an annulment."

Great move on her brother's part, but then

again, he did not expect anything less. The man was dead now, however, and that could seriously delay the processing of an annulment.

He turned to Sir Penforth. "Are you aware that the annulment process will likely be placed on a temporary hold until the murder is solved?"

"Yes, and that is why you are here."

Henry nodded slowly, and returned his attention to the baroness. "How do you feel about your husband's death?"

"He is not my husband," she said slowly and tensely.

"Pardon my address."

"I am not grieving, if that is what you are asking," she continued coolly. "And if you are expecting me to say that I am happy the man who has put me through so much misery is dead, then I am sorry to disappoint you on that front, also."

Henry looked at her for a long moment. He could not begin to fathom her distress and sympathy for her plight grew. But she clearly carried enough anger to push her to commit murder.

"You have a sister yet to be presented to society. How do you think this will affect her?"

"I believe you already know the answer to that question, Detective, and I do not see its relevance to this case."

"It is indeed more relevant than you may think. You will do anything for your sister, won't you?"

"Yes," she admitted slowly as her eyes narrowed. She was obviously a very clever woman. "But I would not commit murder so she can be introduced to society."

"I see." He leaned forward and rested his elbows on his knees. "Do you think Mr. Hart's fate is deserved?"

"Have you not asked me this before?" She was calm. Too calm.

"Yes, but not directly."

"Perhaps I think he should have remained alive to be properly punished for his crimes. And perhaps the manner in which he died is enough punishment." The princess's eyes were cold and hard as she spoke.

Henry was unsure what to believe. She could easily have hired someone to kill the scoundrel who'd taken her. She held enough pain to justify her actions, and her last statement about the manner in which he died could be telling of her capability for murder. That statement was certainly incriminating.

"Have you finished the interrogation?" she asked when he straightened in his chair.

"Yes. I believe you said you have a question for me, too?"

"Not anymore." She jutted her chin forward.

"May I ask why?"

"You do not believe I am innocent. My questions are irrelevant. You will be of no use to me."

Add incredible perception to her list of surprising traits. She was right. He did not think she was innocent. However, he also did not believe she was entirely guilty. He had reached the point where he had to make a decision. Should he take the case and see it to completion?

Instinct guided him and he rose to his feet and addressed Sir Penforth. "Forgive me, but I must decline this case...again."

Sir Penforth shook his head. "I thought you had powerful instincts. I thought it was why you excelled in your work. Clearly, I was mistaken."

He did have powerful instincts. He was hardly ever wrong about people and he had an uncanny ability to read them. But not when it came to Her Royal Highness, Princess Elizabeth Armstrong-Leeds, Baroness Esk. She confused him. He did not know what to make of the woman.

"I wish you the best of luck, Sir." To the princess, he bowed and said, "I am sorry, Ma'am."

She stiffened at the formal address reserved for a princess and turned her head away, refusing to look at him further, and he left the Armstrong-Leeds residence feeling unaccountably muddled.

LIBBY FUMED. HE DIDN'T BELIEVE SHE HAD NOT killed her kidnapper. He was supposed to be shrewd on the investigation front. When he did not believe one to be innocent, he declined in order not to be put in a position that might compromise his integrity. That small aspect of his character was rather admirable. The rest, not so much; he was an arrogant Viscount who had abandoned his family to follow a dream. *Ridiculous man.*

"I am sorry, Libby. I thought he could help."

"I know, Pen. You have done your best." She got to her feet, now more determined than ever to find a way herself to extract her family from this dreadful mess. Pen had done his best and it was time for her to take control of the situation. She was not a murderer and she was going to prove her innocence.

Penforth took her hands in his. "We will get the truth out there, I promise you."

She responded with a small nod and an even smaller smile. When she returned to the drawing room, her mother, sister, and Anna began asking questions as soon as she entered. Libby was almost overwhelmed by them.

"Pen asked Detective DeHavillend to help us with this case, but the detective did not believe I am innocent and has chosen not to take the case."

Her mother slumped back in her chair. "What do we do?"

Anna went to Christiana to try to calm her nerves, while Mary jumped up and came to Libby for a hug.

"You are worried about me," Mary said in a low voice. "Don't be."

Libby's eyes stung and her throat constricted. "How can I not, Mary?"

She held her sister for a long moment before pulling away. "We can always move to England or Europe. Boston is not all there is."

Mary had greatly matured in the past weeks. And she was right; this was not all there was, and they could always move. But that would be a last resort. Libby had to at least try to mend their reputation. Although a fresh start was tempting, Boston would still have a tainted image of them and she would never be completely at ease unless the truth were to be revealed.

"We will be just fine," Mary said.

Libby smiled down at her, feeling encouraged. "Yes, we will be."

She released Mary and went to her mother. "Mama," she said, taking her hand in hers, "it is going to be all right. The police will find the truth."

"What if someone is trying to set you up?" Christiana cried.

Libby had not thought of that possibility. Could that be the case? It gave her an idea of where to start.

"If someone is indeed trying to set me up, I will find them." She stared at Anna and mouthed, "Upstairs," before bringing her attention back to her mother. "Why don't we take you upstairs so you can get some rest."

Christiana nodded. She was a frail woman, not because she had any ailment. She simply did not have as strong a constitution as her son and daughters. Libby was fortunate and thankful she was not like her mother in that regard. She would have crumbled from such a boring existence.

Anna and Libby accompanied Christiana upstairs and gave her some chamomile tea to help her relax before heading to Libby's room where they could talk in private.

"I have an idea," Libby said, propping her foot on a stool to undo the buttons of her boots.

Anna sat on the rose-colored velvet settee at the foot of the bed. "What do we do?"

Libby smiled inwardly at her use of 'we'. She knew Anna would always be there for her. The woman had led her rescue, for heaven's sake.

"Not *we*, just me."

Anna frowned. "What do you mean?"

"I need to find some information and I must go alone." She removed her boots and put them aside, then began undoing the buttons at the neck of her dress.

"I can't let you leave this house alone, Libby," Anna argued, coming up to help her with the buttons she couldn't reach herself. "Not after what you've been through."

Libby turned to face her friend. "Anna, I have never seen Pen this happy in all my life. You mean the world to him and he would kill me if any harm came to you." Anna opened her mouth to speak and Libby quickly held up a silencing finger. "This is something I must do alone. I need you to stay here and take care of Mama and Mary."

Anna frowned. "Only if you tell me where you're going."

Libby turned back so that Anna could continue on the fastenings. "I thought perhaps Sarah might know something. You know what she's like—an ear to the ground all the time. I am going to her premises."

Lady Sarah Smith-Jones was Libby's friend and her favorite clothing designer. She was everyone's favorite designer and moved in both aristocratic, upper and middle-class circles. She also was familiar with a number of people in Boston's underground where illicit business took place. This latter knowledge, however, belonged only to those closest to her, including Libby and Anna. She certainly was not involved in anything untoward herself; she merely had odd connections.

Anna sighed with some relief. "Sarah's shop is in a safe neighborhood. That gives me some comfort."

"I will be fine, Anna. I am much more on my guard now than I was before. Don't worry. Besides, I'm going to wear a disguise."

"Oh?"

Now that her dress was unfastened, she shimmied it off, and moved into her dressing room to retrieve a black satin dress from the back of her closet. It was several years out of fashion, having last been worn to mourn her father. She had forgotten all about it until now.

Holding it against her body, she asked, "What do you think?"

"It's a black dress. Are you disguising yourself as a widow?"

"Precisely! And I *am* a widow now so I suppose this is most fitting," she jested.

"That is not funny, Libby." Anna frowned.

"But it is true."

Anna sighed while Libby retrieved a black lace veil and a black velvet toque. Anna helped her dress and because it had been years since she'd last worn the dress, they had to cinch the corset especially tight. Oh, her aching ribs.

When they were finished, she studied herself in the standing mirror in her dressing room. She doubted anyone who saw her on the streets would recognize her, especially with her face completely concealed by the veil.

"Does it work?" she asked Anna.

"Yes, it does." She smiled. "Very clever."

"I will return before dinner time. If anyone asks, I am tired and asleep in my room."

"Fine. Be careful." Anna hugged her.

Libby did not leave the house through the front door. Instead, she used the servants' entrance on the side of the house. The staff were all busy and she managed to slip out easily. She knew her disguise was working when people on the street carried on with their business without so much as sparing her a glance. Those who did, clearly thought she was a widow.

Libby walked down from her house for about three blocks before hailing a carriage and giving the driver Sarah's shop address. Just as she climbed up into the carriage, she had the strange sensation of being watched. She surreptitiously turned her head but didn't see anyone or anything suspicious. Perhaps everything she had been through had made her paranoid. She shook her head, and settled in her seat.

Comparing the sad state in which she had found herself yesterday evening, and even this morning, she could comfortably conclude that she was no longer near tears. Instead it felt as if there was a fire starting inside her that was growing by the minute, a fire that would only be quenched once she proved her innocence. Libby loved this feeling. She stoked it. Crying and wallowing in misery made her feel pathetic and angry with herself, but this…this assured her she was still in control and that her life was hers to do with as she saw fit.

It didn't take long to reach her destination. The carriage stopped right in front of Sarah's premises: *La Robe Dorée*. Libby liked the name; it was French for The Golden Dress. She paid the driver and even tipped him, then walked up the short staircase to the door.

As her hand touched the door handle, that feeling of being watched crept back. The hairs on the back of her neck rose up.

CHAPTER FOUR

*W*hen Henry left the Armstrong-Leeds house, he headed straight to the Boston Police Department, telling himself he was only going to obtain the bare modicum of information and not become involved. The police station as always was bustling with activity when he arrived.

"Anderson," he greeted the officer at the front desk. He was a genial fellow who lacked the austerity that most police officers had. Henry quite liked him.

"Detective DeHavillend, how is it going?" Anderson asked.

"Good. Is Montgomery in?"

The officer nodded and waved him through. As

Henry turned to find Montgomery, Anderson held him back. "Have you heard?" he whispered.

"Heard what?"

"The kidnapped baroness is now a murder suspect. I heard Chief saying it is so sensitive a case they may have to call you in." He paused with a questioning look in his eyes. "Or have they already called you?"

"Yes, I have heard. No, it is not why I am here. And no, they did not call me."

"Are you going to take the case?"

Henry shook his head. "I don't take cases like that."

Anderson scoffed. "You've taken on worse murder cases."

"Not involving a baroness," he countered before leaving Anderson to search out the District Commander.

Montgomery's office was at the end of a wide hall on the west side of the station and officers who passed Henry paused for perfunctory greetings before moving on. He had the Department's respect, which was unusual for a private detective.

"Ah, just the man I was about to send for," Montgomery said from behind his desk.

"So I've been told," Henry drawled.

Montgomery shook his graying head. "I will need to have a word with Anderson."

"Why are you looking for me?"

"The Armstrong-Leeds case. As if you didn't already know."

Henry held up a hand and shook his head. "I am not getting involved in that. Sir Penforth asked me last night to take the case."

"Did you agree?"

"No."

"Well, we are going to need your help with it. You are the most competent detection expert in this town, outside my department, that is." Montgomery shook his head slowly. "This is a very sensitive case and we must be careful. We are dealing with a baroness here, and a royal too."

"Afraid you will be asked to cover it up?"

Montgomery did not respond and Henry understood. It was one of the reasons he did not generally like working with the police. Many a time, when some shiny Boston Brahmin committed a crime, money changed hands and the crime miraculously disappeared. This annoyed Henry no end.

"If you were afraid of this, then why did you declare her a suspect?"

"There is no one else."

"Not even the deceased's associates?"

"We've caught everyone involved."

"Past victims, perhaps?" Henry suggested.

Montgomery shook his head again. "That is why we need your help."

"Like I said. I am not getting involved."

"Very well," the commander said wearily. "What are you doing here?"

"I want some information about the case."

The commander's eyebrows shot up. "You just said—"

"I know what I said." Henry spoke with some temper. He was unsure why he'd felt the need to come here at all, let alone ask questions about the case. His own actions confused him, and it put him in an ill mood.

The commander's eyes suddenly narrowed with suspicion. "Are you trying to solve this case solo, so you can take all the glory?"

This darkened Henry's mood even further. "Is there anything wrong with that? After all, you do it all the time. I solve your cases and you take the credit. I don't even get paid."

"You will get paid if you work with us…officially."

"Good luck with your case, Montgomery," he

said curtly before turning on his heels and stomping out of the office and building.

The reasonable part of him—the bit that was not confused by the baroness—was quite correct. He should steer clear of this case. Yet the circumstances of it continued to nag at him. *Why?* Was it the case he was unable to stay away from? Or was it *her?*

LOOKING AROUND, LIBBY STILL SAW NO ONE suspicious. She quickly entered the designer's premises. Sarah was crouched by a woman's feet sticking pins into a dress and Libby cleared her throat. Sarah glanced up at Libby but obviously did not recognize her.

"Please have a seat, my lady. I shall be with you shortly. In the meantime, my assistant Camilla will attend to you."

Libby took a seat and waited. When Camilla appeared and offered refreshments, Libby requested a ball pen and paper on which she scrawled a note. The woman Sarah was attending to was known to Libby. Lady Ingrid Bexley was not known for her discretion.

Camilla handed the note to Sarah and she

paused her task to give it a quick read. Her dark head snapped up and her gray eyes widened.

"Lady Bexley, my sincere apologies, but there is something that urgently requires my attention. Camilla can finish the fitting—she is very skilled in that regard."

"No," Lady Bexley began in that dramatic way of hers, flailing her arms and bulging her eyes out as though she had been placed in the most unbelievable situation. "I need this dress tomorrow, and I need it to be perfect."

"These are only minor adjustments and Camilla is more than capable," Sarah said with great patience. "Have I ever disappointed you, Lady Bexley?" When the petulant woman shook her head, she finished with, "Your dress will be perfect. I promise."

The client grumbled but agreed to let Camilla take care of her dress while Sarah quickly pulled Libby to her small office at the rear of the premises.

Sarah pulled her into a tight hug. "I'm so sorry, Libby," she said with great feeling. Then she pulled away. "What are you doing here? And dressed like…*that*?"

"I'm a murder suspect now as you may know."

Sarah nodded. "It is all over town."

"I need to clear my name," Libby said slowly.

"Of course, and I am with you. I wanted to stop by your home later in the afternoon. I have some information that might help."

"You do?"

"Yes." Sarah waved at the settee, and when Libby was settled, sat beside her and continued. "Word is that a hit was put out on Mr. Hart."

"A hit? What is that?"

Sarah laughed lightly. "I forget sometimes that not everyone has led the life I have. At least in recent years. A hit means someone offered money to whoever would kill Mr. Hart."

Libby's eyes widened with surprise, even as she touched her friend's arm, squeezing gently. Sarah's late father was known as an inveterate gambler, and he had lost the family fortune some time back. Sarah had no doubt lived a very different life to the sheltered one Libby knew.

"Do you know who hit my kidnapper?"

"Who put the hit out? Hmm. I suspect it was the proprietor of the worst gambling hell in the city," Sarah's lip curled up with disdain. "A wealthy and reclusive man known as the Raven."

The Raven. She'd never heard that name before.

"Who is he?" Libby asked.

"Not much is known about his past or where

he's from originally, but he is the owner of The Barbican. Have you heard of it?"

Libby gave a nod. The Barbican was an exclusive and prestigious gentlemen's club in the heart of Boston. Pen had a membership there.

"Thank you, Sarah." She was very grateful for this piece of information.

"I had to find something out. I couldn't just sit by and watch my friend accused of murder. I know you didn't do it, Libby." Sarah squeezed her hands.

"I am glad you believe me."

"Always."

"I am going to find this Raven and get to the bottom of this," she declared, preparing to leave.

"I am—unfortunately—slightly acquainted with the man. Would you like me to come with you?"

"Your father's gambling?"

Sarah nodded curtly.

Libby shook her head as she stood. "Thank you, but this is something I have to do alone."

"Of course." Sarah gave her another hug. "Be careful. Don't trust him."

IN UNDER TWO HOURS, LIBBY HAD MADE SOME progress. She had the name—an odd moniker—

and the location of the man who most likely had ordered the death of Mr. Hart. He might also be the one trying to pin the murder on her. She could not wait to share this development with Anna.

She ordered her hired carriage to stop three blocks from home and walked the distance, slipping back into the house the way she had slipped out— through the servants' entrance. She was in her room changing when Anna walked in.

A frown drew her friend's brows together. "I've been worried about you. Did you find anything?"

Libby grinned and opened her arms wide to show Anna that she was absolutely fine. "I did. A man called the Raven put out a hit on Mr. Hart. That is, he ordered someone to kill him. And he may be trying to pin the deed on me."

Anna's blue eyes widened.

"He is the owner of The Barbican and a string of gambling establishments."

"Are you going to tell the police?" Anna asked.

"Not yet. I need to find out more. I intend to visit him."

"Are you certain you should be doing that? If he is trying to pin this on you, then he is most likely very dangerous."

"I'll visit him at one of his clubs. He can't do me any harm in such a public forum."

Anna let out a long sigh. "Just be careful, Libby."

"If I get lost or captured again, at least you will know where to find me," she joked.

"Good Lord! Libby, that is not funny!"

She could not help but laugh at Anna's shocked expression, causing Anna to eventually laugh with her. They needed some levity, even if it was in a painful situation.

"You had best stay out of trouble. I will not go through hell again to find you."

"Nonsense! Of course, you would."

Anna glared at her.

Placing her hand on her friend's shoulder, Libby said, "But it brought you and Pen together."

Anna's expression softened and the fire in her eyes died down as a smile played on her lips. A part of Libby yearned for something like what they had, but she stomped the thoughts as quickly as they broke through the surface of her mind. She was not going there. Absolutely not!

"When do you plan to see the man?" Anna asked.

"Tomorrow afternoon. I don't want to risk going out again today."

"Good."

"How is Mama?"

"She's asleep, and Mary and I were in the drawing room when I heard you return."

"Pen?"

"He is not back from wherever he went earlier."

"I'll change out of this dress and join you for tea."

Anna nodded and left her, and she moved to the window and pulled the heavy red velvet drapes aside. Looking down, her eyes immediately clashed with a set of silver-gray ones staring right up at her window, and her heart jumped.

CHAPTER FIVE

W hy, that wretched man! Was Detective DeHavillend the one who'd been following her? Giving her the goose bumps along her arms as she'd visited Sarah? She *had* felt a presence stalking her while she'd been out. Libby glared down at him and dragged shut the drapes as soon as she caught sight of him standing there in the street. She was still angry with him for not believing that she hadn't committed murder.

And why was she hiding? He was the one in front of her house watching her. She pulled the drapes apart again.

He was still there, standing by a wrought iron fence on the other side of the road. He was wearing a gray greatcoat and a black top hat, and he seemed unperturbed by the autumn drizzle. His silver eyes held hers once again, only this time, she felt her skin tingle. She couldn't deny he had a presence, and even from afar he affected her.

With slow deliberateness, he pulled the brim of his hat down in a greeting gesture and Libby turned away. Now he was mocking her.

She walked into her dressing room and changed her clothes without assistance, then went downstairs. Something made her stop mid-stride in the foyer and she turned toward the front door and opened it very slowly. Surely, he must be gone by now, but she had to check.

Detective DeHavillend was still standing where she had left him, but this time, he was not looking up at her window. He was staring straight at her.

Instead of shutting the door and retreating to the safety of her home, she opened the door wider as their eyes remained locked. She didn't know what it was about him that pulled her, but she did not deny it.

As if he'd heard a silent call, he crossed the street and walked up the short steps to stand before her. She blinked as though she'd just woken from a trance.

"Are you watching me?" she asked, tilting her head back to look at his face. Despite the fact that she was on the step above him, she still had to look up. He was very tall; well over six feet.

"Maybe." One corner of his fine mouth tilted wryly.

Suddenly, she was reminded of her anger toward him. "You didn't want anything to do with my case earlier. Why are you here now?"

"I have not changed my mind, if that is what you are asking."

"No. I'm asking why you're here?"

He shrugged and smiled briefly. "I don't have to answer that," he replied smoothly.

"You are in my house. You have to answer."

His eyes glanced upward. "Technically, I am not *in* your house."

She placed her hands on her hips. "Technically, you have crossed onto my property. So yes, you are in my house."

That lazy smile turned into a proper grin. "You win."

"Why are you here, DeHavillend?"

He laughed now and it irritated her. She could not help but feel mocked. First, he was outside her house watching her, then he was at her front door refusing to tell her why he was here, and now he was laughing at her.

"No Detective?" he asked.

"No. *DeHavillend.*" She stressed his name to return his mockery.

"Fine, *Baroness*. I am here to really find out if you are guilty or not."

She drew in a slow breath and released it. Just what exactly was he playing at?

"I thought you had already decided on my guilt."

He quickly held up a hand. "I never said that."

"You didn't need to."

"I am uncertain," he said, as though he were talking to himself. "I came back to find out more."

"By staring at my window?"

He chuckled and his debonair countenance returned. "I didn't know it was your window. I was trying to determine which window belonged to you when you caught me."

She gave him a dubious look. "You did not look like a man who had just been caught."

"Oh, I don't blush easily." He leaned closer and she caught a waft of his cologne; sandalwood. "However," he added very softly, his voice flowing out and enveloping her with mysterious sensations. "I would like to make *you* blush."

As if he had just commanded them, her cheeks began to heat up. She clenched her jaw and tried to remember all the reasons she disliked him to conceal the effect his closeness had on her senses. "It's not working," she said tersely.

He grinned. "Perhaps you should invite me in for tea and we try again?"

"No, DeHavillend. I am not inviting you into my home."

"What if I want to ask you more questions about the case?"

"I will not let you in even then. And I certainly will not answer any of your questions unless you are officially investigating as my brother earlier asked you to."

He started to dissent and she held up a dismissive hand.

"I no longer want you to investigate my case."

"Are you trying to get back at me for rejecting you the first time?"

Now was Libby's turn to laugh. "What a petty thought!"

The detective was not laughing.

"No, DeHavillend, I am not exacting any sort of revenge," she said, to fill the silence that had fallen. "I have simply reconsidered your involvement in my case and I would rather you don't take it. Faith is very important to me."

"But I hardly know you, Baroness. Asking for faith from me is a bit of a stretch, don't you think?"

He was right, of course, but she would not let him know that. Whether or not he decided to have faith in her, she did not care. She would not allow him to investigate her case and that was final.

"Have a nice day, DeHavillend." She moved fully inside and closed the door in his face. It was rude, she knew, but he seemed to have a talent for bringing out her bad side and making her feel foolish.

"Who was that?" Anna asked from the drawing room doorway.

"Detective DeHavillend," she heard herself say.

Anna brightened. "He wants to take up the case?"

"I don't know what he wants." She shrugged. "I don't want him working on it, though. The man is insufferable."

Her friend nodded, looking slightly deflated. "Tea is ready."

WHAT HAD HE BEEN THINKING? STANDING OUTSIDE her house like that and staring up at her window like some sappy fool. And that conversation at her door? The flirting?

Lord have mercy.

What had come over him?

The baroness was a feisty woman and one of the strongest female personalities he'd ever encountered. He knew this because he had worked on over a hundred complex cases over the years and when a misfortune befell a woman, she usually wailed or swooned or even slipped into incurable melancholy. But Lady Elizabeth did none of that; she was bold and very much in control of herself.

It was this boldness that had him unsure of her innocence, for he believed an innocent woman would soak his handkerchief with her tears.

Right now, with the door slammed in his face, he was still confused.

Henry walked desultorily away, then hailed a passing carriage to take him back to the police station. He didn't care what Montgomery thought of him. He had decided to see this case through. If she was innocent, he would bring the truth to light, and if it were the reverse, justice would be served.

Have faith, she had said. Was that possible, for one such as him?

"Back so soon?" Anderson called when Henry entered the station.

"I have business with Montgomery."

"He said you would return." Anderson chuckled.

Henry rolled his eyes. Montgomery was just leaving and they almost collided. The commander chuckled as he stepped back into his office and invited Henry in. "The look in your eyes said you would not let this go."

Henry did not respond.

"Very few men care about the people involved in a case more than the case itself. Quite a few of my detectives only care about solving the case and earning points. That's not you, is it, DeHavillend? You care about whether or not the woman is innocent."

Henry shrugged. "You should teach your men better. You are, after all, their leader."

Montgomery gave him a rueful smile. "One cannot teach honor, son."

This was perhaps the nicest thing the commander had ever said to him. Instead of feeling good about it, it disturbed him. His own father would rather have died than give him a smile, much less a word of encouragement or praise.

"So, what it is to be? Are you going to help us?" Montgomery asked as he retrieved a folder from his desk and passed it to Henry.

"I am going to help *her*," he corrected, accepting the file.

"That is fine by me."

Henry opened the folder and flipped through the pages containing information about the case. Autopsy results indicated that the most probable cause of Mr. Nolan Hart's death was the blow to his head. But the coroner made no mention of why he reached that conclusion.

"May I see the body?" he asked.

"I don't see why not." The commander moved to the door. "After you."

They left the police station and went into the building next door; a much smaller building. The strong smell of formaldehyde arrested his nose as they approached the coroner's office which was close to the examination room. His stomach turned from both disgust and the stench. This was the part of his job that he liked the least.

Montgomery opened the office door and stepped in first. Mr. Burris, the medical examiner, was bent over his desk scribbling notes onto the page of a large, leather-bound volume. As they approached his desk, Henry realized he was logging records. The chubby man looked up and removed his thick gold-rimmed glasses.

"Good day, Chief, Detective," he greeted. "I assume you are here to see a body."

"That's right," Henry said. "Mr. Nolan Hart."

Mr. Burris picked up a bunch of keys and led them out of his office and into the examination room next-door.

Henry's stomach turned again and he swallowed hard. These were the moments where he had to remind himself of the reason he was doing this. It was the only way to find the fortitude to remain in the room long enough to learn anything.

The coroner directed them to a table and lifted a white sheet from the body. Henry's eyes went straight to the ears where he saw dried blood.

"This is from the blow to the head, correct?" he asked Burris.

"Yes. Bleeding from the ears often indicates heavy trauma. He is more likely to have died from the head injury than the stab wounds."

"And what object do you reckon did this?"

"There is a fracture starting from the occipital bone," Burris pointed at the back of the skull, "all the way to the temporal area. The skull is tough and would require a heavy blow to break."

"Could a woman have done this?"

Burris sighed, looking unsure. "It is possible, yes.

But the question is not the person wielding the object, but the object itself."

Henry interjected, "Mr. Burris, it very much is about the wielder. We have to find the murderer. Can you tell me more?"

"Very well. He was obviously hit from behind and he fell forward. The stab wounds are in the front, so the killer must have turned him over to finish the job. The blow certainly did not kill him instantly."

Henry's eyes went to the multiple slits on the body's torso. They were gruesome and seemed almost...vengeful. Only a severely heartless person could do such a thing.

"One other thing," Burris said. He pointed to the victim's hair. "There is a distinctively perfumed substance on the man's head. Possibly a pomade? There will likely be traces of it on the murder weapon, once it is found."

"I have what I need for now. Thank you, Mr. Burris."

The coroner covered the body and they left the examination room. It was not until Henry and Montgomery were out on the street that Henry bent forward with his hands braced on his knees. He took deep breaths.

"Yes, I can never get used to the chemical smell

myself," Montgomery said, giving Henry an avuncular pat on his back. "But you have it worse than me."

When his stomach was no longer turning and his breathing was even, he straightened. "Is there nothing they can use for preservation instead of that?"

"I doubt there is."

They headed back to the commander's office and closed the door behind them.

"What do you think?" Montgomery asked.

"I don't believe she did it," Henry replied.

"What brought on the change?"

"Only an incredibly vicious person would kill like that; a person without a conscience. She does not seem like she is lacking in that regard," he explained. "But then again, she could have hired a soulless individual to do it, but I suspect she is not the kind to have people take care of her problems." As he spoke, he realized that what he was saying about the baroness was the truth.

His short conversation with her in front of her house had revealed a lot. Her eyes were very expressive when she was not consciously trying to conceal her emotions and her reaction to his flirtation had given him a glimpse of her innocence.

And innocent people did not commit vicious murder.

Montgomery clapped him on the back again. "Well, good luck, son."

He was going to need it. He placed the file back on the desk and left the police station, turning over his next plan in his mind as he went.

CHAPTER SIX

L ate afternoon seemed like the best time to visit The Barbican. Sarah had told her that the Raven was almost always there, as he preferred the place to the other gentlemen's clubs in his retinue.

Libby dressed as she had the day before, in black and hidden behind a veil, and slipped out of the house after informing the others that she was going up for an afternoon nap. She even pretended to be feeling faint from the stress the situation was causing her.

The truth was that she was feeling more determined than stressed. Her blood rushed with adrenaline every time she was out on a quest. Like now.

She was not afraid of danger. Not when she

was on the lookout for it. It was this fearlessness that had landed her in trouble before, but she was far more cautious now…at least, she tried to be. She now carried a sheathed blade in the pocket of her dress and a small gun strapped to her thigh beneath her skirts. She would be foolish to allow what happened to her three weeks ago to happen again.

She walked down the street, the confidence from her disguise brightening her mood. It was thankfully not raining despite the grayed skies. Boston had not seen sunshine in days and the hornbeam trees on the streets had been stripped almost completely of their leaves.

The sound of her boots on the cobblestones created a smooth rhythm, but as she passed the second block, the clicking of another pair of shoes joined hers and she instantly became more alert. She didn't turn to find out who was following her. She only listened and pulled the lapels of her short black cloak more tightly about her body.

Someone was following her again. Quickening her steps, she half jogged the rest of the distance to the carriage station where she had hailed a ride yesterday. The same carriage that had transported her to Sarah's shop was waiting on the side of the road. She turned to see if she was still being followed and by whom, but again, saw nothing out of the ordinary.

Libby shook her head. No, this could not be paranoia. She was not in so much of a muddle that she was beginning to imagine danger where it did not exist. She was certain of those footsteps she'd heard and the presence she had felt. A shiver ran through her and she hurried across the street to the waiting carriage.

She gave the driver the address and climbed in, turning one last time to look about her. Whoever was following her was adept at stalking, and as much as she had cause to believe it was Detective DeHavillend, she did not think it was him. This felt ominous and fearful, quite like a predator stalking its prey.

And Libby felt like the prey.

Another shiver ran through her and she hugged her arms around her as the carriage jolted into motion.

In twenty minutes, they rolled to a halt in front of a grand building that combined Victorian and Grecian architecture. It was in a quiet neighborhood with streets that were almost empty. That was understandable, given gentlemen usually visited clubs in the evening. She could easily imagine the line of grand carriages that would fill this street by nightfall.

She stepped out and looked up at the building. Sculpted scrollwork rimmed the roof and separated the floors. Tall columns stood on either side of the front door and were replicated on the terraces on the upper floors directly above the entrance.

She took a tentative step forward then paused to think. She had half a mind to turn around and go home, but she had come this far. And if she was any closer to finding the truth, she could not turn back now.

With a deep breath, she lifted her veil, stepped up to the front door, and pulled the knocker. A man —a steward from what she could tell—stepped out and looked her over with contempt.

"Yes?" he asked in a haughty manner.

"I am here to see the owner of this establishment."

The man looked her over again and she suddenly began to feel self-conscious.

"We do not admit women into this establishment."

His comment hit a nerve. She and Anna had been fighting against gender inequality for a long time. This was a public place—albeit exclusive—and she saw no reason why a woman should not be allowed entry. They were human too and entitled to just as much freedom as men. But society was unfair.

"Do you know to whom you are speaking?" She raised her voice a notch.

He glared at her with a mixture of boredom and disdain.

"I am Baroness Esk and my brother, His Royal Highness, Prince Penforth Armstrong-Leeds, has membership here."

"That means nothing to me." The steward shrugged. "I have no proof that you are who you say you are, and besides, you are a *woman*. We do not admit women. Not even the First Lady."

A brawny man appeared behind the steward and whispered something in his ear. The man stepped aside and the hulk came to stand in front of her. Libby's heart sped up.

"You are the muscle here, aren't you?" she asked. "Perhaps you will be more reasonable than your colleague."

"Leave!" he barked.

Libby's eyes widened. *Well. So much for reasonable.* "Look—"

He took a menacing step toward her. "If you don't leave, I will throw you in front of that carriage coming this way."

She turned to see a carriage rolling toward them. She had to find a way to placate this man. Clearly, invoking Pen's name was not an option.

"Listen," she began, keeping her voice even. "I am—"

Before she could register what was happening, the man picked her up and threw her down the steps and onto the road. The carriage was almost upon her.

Henry saw the baroness leave the Armstrong-Leeds House. Something about her furtive manner drew his attention in the first instance, and within seconds he realized it was her because of the graceful way she moved. He followed, wondering why the obstinate woman had snuck out dressed like a widow.

Surprisingly, someone else began to follow her, too. He sped up but they turned into an alleyway and disappeared. He had to choose between following them and her. He chose to hail a carriage and asked the driver to follow her. She seemed oblivious to the dangers around her and his ire grew.

Did she really think a heavy black dress, a cloak,

a hat, and a veil were a good disguise? She would have been better off wearing men's clothing.

When they arrived at their destination, he stopped several meters away and assessed the situation. What the devil was she doing at The Barbican?

He began to close the distance between them as she exchanged words with the doorman. Then a large man came out and took over. Henry began to run, concern taking hold. Before he could reach her, the giant grabbed her and threw her onto the road where the carriage he had just alighted from was passing.

Henry's entire body ignited and he raced as fast as he could, his heart threatening to burst out of his chest. His vision was a complete blur. All he could see was a pile of black in the middle of the road and horse hooves and wheels coming ever closer.

He dove forward and landed on top of her, covering her body with his before rolling with her out of the carriage's way. Her head was cradled against his chest and her body was trembling. So was he.

Henry remained there with her in his arms until he had regained his composure...some of it, for he was very angry. With her, and with the man who had pushed her...*especially* with her. She would not have been pushed if she had remained in the safety of her home.

He pulled away, rose to his feet which felt rather weak, and helped her up. A gasp escaped her lips when she saw him.

"DeHavillend!"

"What were you thinking?"

She was still visibly disoriented, but managed a fiery response. "I am close to finding out who really killed the man who kidnapped me."

"And you think coming out alone is the way to go about it? You were almost killed just then!"

Her amber eyes flared at him. "If you think I should stay home like some delicate flower lamenting my situation into a pretty lace handkerchief, then you are gravely mistaken! The police want to take me into custody and men like you do not believe that I did not kill him!"

"I offered to take the case yesterday and you rejected me. You should have allowed me to take care of things."

"You do not believe me!" She shouted the words at him, and Henry was silenced. He did believe her, now. Not just because of her outburst, but because she was obviously willing to risk her life in order to clear her name. A guilty person would not take that action.

He felt somewhat ashamed.

While they were squabbling, the club door suddenly opened. Henry turned to find the steward walking toward them. The man first bowed to the baroness and then to Henry.

"My sincere apologies, Sir. My master would like to see you." He looked at the baroness. "You most especially, my lady."

The Baroness glared at him. "Why? A moment ago, your hulking friend tried to kill me."

The steward bowed his head. "You earned his respect. Not many women will challenge the Raven's guards. You didn't back down."

The baroness sniffed and huffed for a moment, before straightening her delicate shoulders and marching forward. One corner of Henry's mouth tilted up in admiration of her poise and grace, before he quickly followed her.

LIBBY WAS STILL VERY SHAKEN OVER HER NEAR-death encounter, but she put forth her best posture and most stoic countenance. She was in the realm of men now and any show of vulnerability, however small, could not be afforded. She pictured them like wolves poised to attack; one wrong move and they would rip her to shreds.

She brushed past the despicable steward and into The Barbican. If she were here under different circumstances, today would go down in history as the day the most exclusive and prestigious club in Boston admitted its first woman.

She was greeted by the smell of cigars and liquor. It was a comforting smell, somewhat like Pen's study at home. The front hall was decorated in the darkest shades of brown, giving the place a dark and mysterious air. They climbed two flights of stairs and turned down a wide hallway, also decorated in browns. The scent of a strong cologne filled the air and intensified as they approached their final destination—a salon with an elegant coffered ceiling and paneled walls. To her relief, the entire room was not decorated in varying shades of brown. The drapes were sage green and the carpet was olive green and ivory, while the massive fireplace was black marble.

It was all very masculine. She would bet the place would look far more welcoming if it had a woman's touch.

A tall, dark-haired man stood looking out one of the windows and when he heard them enter, he turned. He must be the Raven. His deep green eyes glittered dangerously as they roved Libby, not in a condescending manner, but in an admiring one. His mouth was curved up at one corner and he moved with languid grace.

"Welcome, Baroness Esk," he greeted with a courtly bow. When he straightened, he gave DeHavillend an acknowledging nod before waving them toward a sitting area in front of the fireplace. "Please, sit."

She lowered herself onto a brown leather sofa. DeHavillend sat beside her and her senses awakened to his closeness. Despite the smell of cigar and heavy cologne in the air, she could still perceive the detective's subtle sandalwood scent and her nostrils flared in response, strangely wanting more.

She twisted her head and found his silver gaze on her, but it was not inquiring or amused as it usually was. It was stern and focused. He was still angry with her, she could feel it, but at the same time, she sensed his protectiveness.

A warm feeling was just beginning to swirl around her when the Raven spoke, breaking the spell.

"My deepest apologies for the way my men handled you. I will see they learn from this. Ladies should not be treated in that manner."

She nodded her acceptance of the apology and folded her gloved hands on her lap, waiting for him to continue.

"Would you like something to drink?" he asked.

"No, thank you," she said stiffly.

"A whiskey for me," DeHavillend requested.

The Raven raised his hand slightly to call the attention of a footman waiting by the door. "Our finest whiskey for Detective DeHavillend…"

Her eyes narrowed in question. The detective had not given anyone his identity since their arrival.

The Raven smiled rakishly. "I know a lot of things, my lady." Then he turned back to the footman. "A bourbon for me and wine for the baroness."

"Certainly not!" she interjected firmly.

CHAPTER SEVEN

"**Y**ou will do well not to assume what I drink." She looked at the footman then. "I will have what the detective is having."

Henry's brows did a slow ascent and he felt his lips curving upward. She never failed to surprise and bewilder him. And from the look on the Raven's face, he had not been expecting that, either.

The footman bowed politely and left to retrieve their drinks.

"So, my lady, to what do I owe the pleasure of your presence?"

"Oh, quit pretending," she said, rolling her eyes. "We both know you find no pleasure in my visit. You have just admitted a woman into your establishment for the first time, and if the ego you're oozing is any indication, you will do all you can to keep that fact hidden."

Henry knew the Raven, at least by reputation, and he smiled into his hand at Lady Elizabeth's comment. This was definitely not the first time a woman had been admitted into The Barbican. But certainly, it might be a first for a lady. She clearly did not know that, of course. Why should she? This was not part of her world.

"My dearest Baroness," the Raven drawled in an ironic tone, "you are not the first female to set foot in The Barbican. It is not something I need to hide."

"Good. Then perhaps you should consider giving women membership."

He chuckled darkly. "Society has not reached that point yet, my lady. But I assure you that if it ever does, I will happily offer women membership to The Barbican."

"Shouldn't something as relevant as social inequality trump your desire to stay in business?" she challenged.

The man's eyes flared with something like admiration. Henry understood that emotion. Lady Elizabeth was proving to be an impressive young woman and she had somehow crawled into his mind and wedged herself there.

"I am certain you have not come all the way here to convince me to admit women into my establishment. What can I do for you, my lady?"

Just then the steward returned with their drinks. His master dismissed him and closed the door firmly behind him on exit. Henry took a small sip of his drink and allowed it to burn a trail down his throat, invigorating him.

Libby spoke. "I have information that the Raven put out a hit on Mr. Nolan Hart. You *are* the Raven, are you not?"

Their host's eyes narrowed to slits. "Who gave you that information?"

"That is irrelevant. Did you or did you not have Mr. Hart killed?"

"It is relevant to me." His eyes gleamed dangerously. "I want to know who is dragging my name through the dirt."

Lady Elizabeth stiffened slightly and reached for her drink. "For their protection, I would rather not tell you," she said, taking a sip of her whiskey and coughing slightly. "Better not have another body turn up in a ditch outside of town."

"I am not sure if you are brave or stupid." The Raven studied her and Henry stiffened, ready to jump to her aid. He relaxed a little when the man added, "Perhaps you are both. I take no responsibility for Mr. Hart's death." He raised his snifter to his lips, but changed his mind and lowered it before leaning forward. "The police are after *you* for the murder, are they not?"

"Yes."

"I would not blame you if you truly did kill him. The man was trouble for everyone. I can tell you he had many enemies."

He leaned back in his chair and picked up his glass once again.

Henry observed him. For all his reputation for being dark and dangerous, the Raven did not give off the air of a man who was lying.

"Are you certain you did not have him killed?" Lady Elizabeth asked.

"I think he is telling the truth," Henry offered. His gut told him he was correct.

The Raven raised his glass as if in a toast. "If you don't believe me, then perhaps you will believe your detective."

She shrugged, and then raised her drink to her lips and took a generous swig, shutting her eyes briefly at the burn. That action was the only clue to her distressed state.

After a moment her composure returned. "If it

wasn't you, then do you have any information about the possible killer?"

"I am sorry, my lady, but I have nothing for you."

She rose to her feet gracefully and inclined her head in a regal manner. "Thank you for your time, Sir."

The Raven rose to his feet as well. "I wish you luck, Baroness." He turned his gaze to Henry. "You too, Sir."

The steward showed them out of The Barbican. When outside, Henry took her gloved hand and tucked it in the crook of his elbow. She did not resist and a warm feeling curled through him. "I will see you home myself," he said as they began walking down the street.

"I do not need a bodyguard," she responded.

"I know you are capable, but sometimes we need a little extra help."

She was staring straight ahead when she said, "I don't need your help, DeHavillend."

"Nevertheless, I insist on giving it."

Her huffed out breath carried annoyance.

"You are angry with me," he stated.

"No."

"Yes, you are."

She stopped and turned to face him before

releasing a sigh. "You are the least of my problems right now. I don't have the time or luxury to be angry with you. I just lost my only lead."

He closed his eyes at the broken look in her eyes. He wanted to pull her against him and comfort her, but was certain she would not allow it.

"I do believe you, Lady Elizabeth," he murmured.

She continued walking. "You pity me," she said. "That is why you claim to believe me now."

"That's not true. My interactions with you yesterday and today have given me a glimpse of who you truly are. I have been doing this a long time, and I know you are not a murderer."

She did not dignify his statement with a response and it stung him somewhat. So much so, that he was forced to stop and turn her to face him. He placed his hands firmly on her shoulders to prevent her from escaping.

"Forgive me," he said, hoping she could see that he was sincere. "It was not my intention to upset you. I was uncertain of your innocence and you are a high-born lady, a royal in fact. I did not want to have to cover up a crime if you were found guilty and your family demanded your image be kept clean. That goes against my sense of right or wrong."

Her expression softened.

"Let me help you, Lady Elizabeth. Let me help you bring the truth to light."

She released a shaky breath and nodded. He placed her hand back into the crook of his elbow, even more protectively this time, and found them a carriage to take her home.

DeHavillend walked her to the same side entrance she'd left from. The sun had gone down and his face was shadowed by the darkness, but she was still able to make out his features, especially those silvery eyes.

He had offered to help her, but she still was unsure about his motives. Was he doing this for his own personal gain? Money, perhaps? No, it couldn't be that. He hailed from a very wealthy family and although his reason for giving up a life of luxury was beyond her understanding; she was certain he did not need money.

Glory? Perhaps he wanted to appear a hero. But everyone knew Detective DeHavillend did not work for glory. If anything, the police took all the credit whenever he worked with them.

In the end, she straight out asked. "What do you stand to gain from helping me?"

"I don't know," he said simply.

"There has to be a reason. You can't just help me for nothing."

He looked down at her for a long moment but didn't say anything. There *was* something, she could tell, but he did not seem inclined to share.

"You can come inside and discuss the matter with my brother if you want to officially take on the case."

He shook his head slowly. "I am not accepting a contract."

"Why not?"

Again, he did not respond, and this time, Libby understood. "You want to leave things open so you can walk away at any time, don't you?"

A flicker of something in his eyes told her that she was right and she momentarily reveled in the satisfaction it brought her.

"I will help you in any way I can and that is what matters."

He was a rather strange man. She did not understand him one whit.

"Fine. What do you propose I do now that I am back right where I started?"

"You will stay put in your home, and I will scout for more information."

Was he being serious? "Have you heard nothing I said earlier?" She wanted to smack him on the head with something so his senses could return to him…if he had any, to begin with.

He gave her a sly smile. "You will not stay home like some delicate flower lamenting your situation into a pretty lace handkerchief."

She opened her mouth to say something but for the life of her, she did not know what, so she closed it.

"I see you have trouble letting go of your power so I am not asking you to stay home and do nothing. I am only asking you to stay home until I can find another lead."

"And how long might that take?"

"I am uncertain."

"All right," she said.

His eyes narrowed. He was right to be suspicious. She had no intention of *staying put* while he hunted for information. But she had to make him believe otherwise. It was the only way she could get him to stop following her.

"Good night, DeHavillend. And thank you for rescuing me earlier." She had to give him credit where it was due. Those horse hooves had been very close indeed.

"My pleasure, Baroness. I will see you soon."

She gave him one last glance and slipped into the house. Like a thief in the night, she removed her boots before slowly creeping up the stairs to her room.

What a day!

Libby moved to her window and slowly pulled the edges of the velvet drapes apart just a little. He would not be there, she was sure, but she wanted to check, nevertheless…just to sate her curiosity.

And sate it she did, for he stood on the street near the wrought iron fence looking up at her. Instead of ducking like she did last time, she opened the window and poked out her head.

He grinned and somehow, she found herself grinning back. It felt, for a moment, as if they were embarking together on an adventure.

"What are you still doing here?" she asked in a loud whisper.

He crossed the street and walked closer, stopping right beneath her two floors below.

"Don't you have somewhere to be, DeHavillend?"

"There's a whiskey snifter in the Algonquin with my name on it, but I rather like it here."

Libby bit back another grin.

"Go home."

"Who are you talking to?" Mary's voice came from behind her.

Libby quickly pulled the shutters and stepped out from behind the curtain. "No one," she yelped. "I…err…I was acting out a scene from a play."

"What?" Her sister frowned.

"*Romeo and Juliet.* Remember when Juliet looked out from her terrace at Romeo?" She kept her tone even.

"Right…" Mary said, looking somewhat puzzled. "I was heading down for dinner and I saw the light under your door." Her eyes then did a slow assessment of Libby from her black toque down to her toes. "What are you wearing?"

Good heavens!

"I am rewriting Shakespeare's play. Romeo is dead and Juliet is alive. She is his widow now."

"Libby," Mary said with great concern and walked over to her, taking her hands. "I know this is really hard for you, but the marriage will be annulled and you will be free."

"What has this to do with my play?"

"Well, you are married and the man…I-I'm sorry." Mary's hands went up to cover her face.

Oh, Lord! Now her sister thought she was going

mad and unable to tell if she was playing her real-life role as a widow.

"Mary," she said softly as she pulled the girl's hands from her face. "I am all right. I am just playing to take my mind off things."

Her sister nodded. "That's understandable, I suppose. We all need an outlet sometimes."

"Precisely. Now, go. I'll join you once I change."

AFTER DINNER, LIBBY SAT WITH ANNA IN THE library. Her friend was staying with them because her mother was still abroad, and though Anna was used to running Wrexford House on her own, they all enjoyed her company. Especially Pen.

"How did it go with the Raven?" Anna whispered.

"He is not responsible."

Anna gave her a dubious look. "Are you sure? Is that what he made you believe?"

"Well, Detective DeHavillend was there—"

"Detective DeHavillend?"

Libby ignored her surprised question and continued. "He believes—the detective, that is—he believes the Raven is telling the truth."

Anna shook her head. "I am lost. You went there with the detective?"

"No, he followed me." Libby deliberately left out the bit where she was attacked and thrown in front of a carriage. Her family was worried enough as it was.

"For a man who wants nothing to do with this case, he certainly does hang around you a lot." There was a sliver of irony in Anna's tone which caused Libby to suspect she knew something.

She raised an enquiring brow, and Anna gestured at the window. The library window, that happened to be directly beneath Libby's bedroom. "I saw him out there earlier."

Libby rolled her eyes in a show of indifference. "I can't seem to get him to stop following me."

"What are you going to do now?"

"I don't know, Anna. I am back where I started."

"I can't think of anything, either," her friend admitted.

"We could always leave town," she said with a rueful smile. "You know, start over."

Anna reached over on the sofa they were sharing to give her hand a pat. "We'll find a way out of this."

She hoped Anna was right.

CHAPTER EIGHT

THE BARBICAN

*H*enry lowered himself into a dark leather chair beside the sofa he had sat on with Lady Elizabeth earlier that day. It was now nearing midnight, and he should be home trying to get some much-needed sleep. Instead, he was back here at The Barbican in another audience with the Raven.

"You never rest, DeHavillend, do you?"

"Not when there is a murderer on the loose."

The Raven smiled noncommittally. "So, what can I do for you?"

"I believe you know more than you let on, today."

"I told you I have nothing."

Henry reached into his coat pocket and retrieved a folded paper. He slid it across the table to the man opposite. It was a neat copy of one of the statements in the murder case.

After leaving the Armstrong-Leeds House, he went back to the police station, locked himself in Montgomery's office, and perused the entire contents of the case file. He was searching for anything he might have missed, and he did find something.

He waited for the other man to finish reading the contents of the paper before he spoke. "That shows that Mr. Hart was here just hours before his death."

"An officer from the police department has already questioned me. It is all here in this record."

It was true that a police officer had visited The Barbican to investigate after word had reached them about Mr. Hart's attendance here just hours before his death. Interesting that the Raven had not mentioned that earlier, nor had he provided any relevant information to the investigation.

"I am not the police." Henry leaned back in his seat, wishing he had chosen to go home instead. It had been a rather long and eventful day and his thoughts swirled in useless circles.

The Raven studied him carefully.

"I am *not* the police," Henry repeated, and after a moment, the other man seemed to relent.

"Very well. I assume I can rely on your discretion?"

At Henry's nod, the Raven continued. "Nolan Hart owed me a great deal of money and I summoned him to discuss the matter."

"Let me hazard a guess. You threatened him."

The Raven shrugged. "I am a businessman, DeHavillend. And I have a reputation to uphold."

It was making more sense now. "You did not send an assassin after him but someone used the threat you made to put word out that you did. The lead Baroness Esk followed."

The Raven raised his glass as if in a toast. "It would seem so."

"*Would* you have sent someone after him?" Henry asked.

The man stroked his chin as if in deep thought. "If I had, I would not have allowed it to be so..." He wrinkled his nose before finishing. "Gruesome. Or final. Makes it much more difficult to recover a debt if the man is dead, don't you agree? A threat? Perhaps. But murder? No. Not useful at all."

That made a wicked kind of sense. Henry had no cause to doubt the man, but he was going in circles with this case. Right now, he was lost as to how to proceed. He rubbed his eyes.

"Twisted case, yes?"

Henry let out a small frustrated laugh. "Indeed. Thank you for the information," he said, and then rose to leave.

"You have not touched your whiskey," his host remarked.

Henry looked down at the finger of liquid in the glass. "I am far too tired."

With that, he left The Barbican and headed home.

ARMSTRONG-LEEDS HOUSE

The following morning

THE BUTLER SHOWED HENRY TO A DRAWING ROOM where Lady Elizabeth was waiting. One look at her had his thoughts scattering all over again and the impulse to get close to her returned, overwhelming him.

The pale yellow and white day dress she was wearing lent her an air of innocence while keeping her green-amber eyes sharp and very lovely. Her lustrous dark hair was not piled atop her head in the usual fashion. Instead, she had styled it in a loose knot at her nape with soft curly locks falling over her shoulder and some framing her face. Her bruises were hardly visible now and he was glad that she seemed to be healing nicely.

The first time he had seen those bruises, anger had coursed through him. Any man who would raise his hand to a woman was a beast. Lady Elizabeth was a slight woman with delicate features, but he had quickly learned that her will was stronger than steel.

"DeHavillend," she greeted him in the same abrupt manner as his male associates.

If he were not investigating her case, he would have crossed the room to where she sat, given her a courtly bow, then taken her hand and placed a soft kiss on her knuckles. He could still do that, if he wished, but it felt improper in the circumstances.

"Henry," he said. "Please call me Henry. I believe we are past the point of formal address."

She pursed her lips, drawing his gaze to them; soft and full and pretty. "I suppose you are right. You may call me Elizabeth, if you wish, although I would much prefer Libby."

He smiled at her, feeling a sudden closeness

despite the space between them. "Do all your friends call you Libby?"

"Just those I am closest to."

He sat in a chair adjacent to her and regarded her carefully. "Do you consider me a close friend, then?"

"We are hardly friends, but I do believe you are someone I can trust."

"Trust," he said, measuring the word on his tongue. "You feel you can trust me, but we are not friends."

She shook her dark head.

Henry held out his hand to her. "Can we not have both friendship and trust?"

She hesitated for a long time before finally accepting his hand. He had intended the contact to be a brief handshake—one of acquaintances becoming friends—but he grasped her fingers and let the sensation flow through him, warm and tender and unexpected.

He was treading a dangerous path, he knew, but it was too late now. Libby—he quite liked how the name sounded in his mind—did things to him that he could not understand. It was time he stopped fighting against the effect.

"You have something for me?" Her soft voice broke into his musing.

"Oh. Yes, I do." He released her and shifted in his chair. "I went back to The Barbican to meet with the Raven late last night."

Her brows drew together. "Why?"

"I re-checked the case file at the police department and found out that the last place Mr. Hart visited before his death was The Barbican." Her eyes widened hopefully as she straightened in her seat. "Apparently, he owed the Raven quite a bit of money and he had been summoned to either pay or confirm arrangements to do so forthwith."

"It seems the owner of The Barbican has a motive, too."

"Yes, but it turns out he didn't do it."

She seemed disappointed and Henry understood why. She had hoped something else would arise that would take the blame off her.

"How does this information help us?"

"It is true that the Raven threatened him and someone must have heard. Who gave you the information about the hit?"

Her expression quickly shuttered. "A friend."

"A friend?"

"I can't tell you who, Henry. Surely, you must understand my reason. I can't endanger them."

"I do understand," he said in a soothing tone. "Do you know where they got the information?"

"No, but they're not one to tell lies."

"Can you ask them?"

"Yes, of course. I can go there today."

"I believe someone is playing at something behind the scenes. Misdirection everywhere—first toward you, and now the Raven. Finding out who is doing the misdirecting, might lead us to the killer."

Libby's eyes brightened. "Truly?"

Henry nodded. "I will leave you now, but we should meet again soon." He got to his feet and she rose from her chair.

"Thank you, Henry," she said quietly, sincerely.

Henry had to check to make sure his hands were firmly at his sides as they should be. The urge to touch her was almost too much. With a curt nod in her direction, he stalked out of the room as quickly as he was able to. The butler who had received his greatcoat and hat was nowhere to be found, unfortunately.

He swiveled and found Libby in the drawing room entrance with a puzzled look on her face.

"My coat. I gave it to the butler."

She crossed the hall to open a door and slip inside—the cloakroom, perhaps. When she reappeared, she had his coat and hat with her.

"I would ask you why you are in such a hurry to

leave, but I suspect you would not give me a straight answer."

"You are coming to know me already," he murmured as he collected his things from her.

"You are not the only one with the gift of reading people, Henry."

He quirked a smile. "I am starting to see that."

THE JOURNEY TO SARAH'S SHOP FELT LONGER THIS time, but then, Libby was anxious to arrive. She was in such a hurry to climb down from the carriage that she almost forgot her black-beaded reticule on the seat.

Thankfully, there was only one client in Sarah's premises and it looked like they had just concluded their business.

"Did you find him?" Sarah asked as soon as they were alone.

"Yes, but it seems as if he didn't do it, either."

If Libby didn't know better, she would think that was relief that just crossed her friend's face. She dismissed the thought as ridiculous, and carried on with what she had come for. "Where did you get the information about the hit, Sarah?"

"A man who supplies me with Belgian lace also

supplies liquor to The Barbican. I heard it from him."

"What is his name?" she asked urgently.

"Terrance Read."

"Do you know where I can find him?"

Sarah penned down an address on a piece of paper, folded it, and gave it to Libby who nodded her thanks.

"I'm glad I could help," Sarah said. "But really, what is going on, Libby?"

"It appears someone is spreading rumors; giving false trails. We think tracking down that person will lead us to the true killer and I can finally clear my name."

"Oh, please be careful. And remember that I am here if you need anything," Sarah assured her.

Libby was glad she had such supportive friends. It marked her as a very fortunate lady, despite the current circumstances.

She left *La Robe Dorée* and studied the address on the paper. Roxbury. It was not the safest of neighborhoods, but she did not want to drag Anna to a place like that and asking Pen to go with her was not an option. He would take over, for sure.

And Henry? It felt quite strange thinking of him by his Christian name. For some reason she hesitated to call on him. When Henry was around, her feelings were all aflutter and she had trouble thinking straight. Perhaps it would be all right to check this out on her own, and then call upon Henry to assist should any additional leads come to light. I can do this, she thought. I don't need Henry to hold my hand.

Libby's heart sped up. Roxbury was a fast-growing area and a good place for merchants and businesses, but it was not free of crime. Footpads often attacked the upper-class who dared venture out after nightfall, and there had been murders and other crimes often centered around the debauched gambling dens that had made the neighborhood infamous.

But she had to brave it, if she wanted to find out the truth.

CHAPTER NINE

BOSTON POLICE DEPARTMENT

"*A* witness came forward early this morning." Montgomery handed Henry the case file. "On the last page."

Henry opened to the page and read the witness report.

A lady fitting Libby's description had bashed Mr. Hart on the head with a boulder and then stabbed him. The witness claimed to have seen a carriage stop on the side of the road in a street in Roxbury after midnight on the day the murder had occurred. Mr. Hart had come out of a bar staggering and appeared drunk. A woman had alighted from the carriage and walked up to him before they had a heated conversation. She pulled him into a nearby alley where she killed him. Afterward, someone else came to cart the body away.

Henry found many things wrong with the witness's statement.

"Who is the witness?"

"A lady. For her safety, we are keeping her anonymous," Montgomery replied.

"A proper lady?"

Montgomery nodded.

"I see you are still keeping information from me." The police did not share everything and sometimes they dangled information before him like a carrot on a stick to entice him to join them.

"You know we can't. Besides, I took the statement myself, so only I know who she truly is. If you want full information, you will have to become one of us."

Never.

Henry dismissed that with an uncaring wave of his hand. "You said the witness is a *lady*."

"Yes."

"In Roxbury, after midnight. Montgomery, do you not find anything wrong with both the witness and the statement?" Henry gave the commander a disbelieving look.

"That is why I called you in."

Irritated, Henry snapped the folder shut. "So, you are letting me do all the work."

"Let me be honest with you, son. We have many reservations regarding this case. We are dealing with a very influential family here."

A bitter laugh escaped his throat. "That is cowardly."

"Maybe it is. You may no longer feel as you did earlier, but we are still looking for a murderer. If she is found guilty, it will be a shame to cover this up."

"Then don't!" Henry snapped.

Montgomery was quiet for a very long time with his eyes fixed on the folder in Henry's hands. "It is not that simple, DeHavillend."

"So you just stay out of it? *That* is your way of bringing justice to the city?"

The commander did not respond, and Henry sighed. Instead of attacking the police about what they were doing wrong, perhaps he should focus even more energy into solving this case. "She didn't do it," he stated.

Montgomery's brows rose. "The witness report—"

"Is full of holes."

Tugging down his uniform coat and removing

lint from his sleeve, Montgomery said, "Take a seat and we'll work out the holes."

Henry did as requested, and opened the file again, this time removing the paper containing the witness's statement completely.

"What was a lady doing in Roxbury at midnight?" he asked again.

"That is a good question."

"Have you confirmed Lady Elizabeth's alibi?"

"She told Graves that she was asleep at that time."

Confirming her alibi would be difficult given the time the murder had been deemed to occur. Libby did have a knack for stealing out of the house.

"And she said the body was taken away in a cart…"

"What do you say we check the street, maybe ask a few people some questions?" Montgomery suggested.

Henry nodded. "Excellent idea."

As they exited the commander's office, Anderson came rushing down the hall. "You are needed in the mayor's office, Chief."

Montgomery sighed and looked apologetically at Henry. "You are going to have to go ahead without me, son."

"That is fine."

"Let me know what you find." With that, the commander left with Anderson and Henry hailed a carriage and made for Roxbury.

HER FOOT LANDED IN A PUDDLE AND SANK UP TO her ankles, drenching the hem of her dress.

But Libby didn't care. If she wanted to keep her clothes clean and her boots dry, she would not have come here.

Terrance Read's shop should be on this street. As she looked around at the brick buildings and colorless surrounds, her stomach flipped.

Do not be afraid, she told herself as she took a deep steadying breath.

The building before her was number seven, she realized, and her destination was number seventeen. The carriage had dropped her at least a hundred yards from Terrance Read's shop. She huffed in frustration and wanted to stamp her foot on the ground like a child about to throw a tantrum. But that would only get her muddier, and blaming the carriage driver would not change anything.

She took a tentative step forward, taking note of her surroundings, every building, every face. The streets were busy and the bustle almost gave her a sense of security, but she knew better than to rely on the kindness of strangers when she found herself in trouble.

When she had been kidnapped, she had been taken to a chapel where she had been forced to marry Mr. Hart. On seeing the minister, Mr. Anders, she had hoped that he would help her. He had been just as bad, locking her up in a dank crypt without food or water for quite some time. He had also hit her across the face many times.

Libby paused and clenched her teeth together while she balled her hands into fists to suppress the memories. The very air in this place smelled of despondency and as if the heavens wanted to demonstrate the gloom, they opened up and sent an untimely downpour.

She opened her umbrella and quickened her steps. If she got lost, at least Sarah would know she had been headed here and Anna knew she had gone to see Sarah.

Right now, as she walked quickly toward Terrance Read's shop, she became aware of that presence that seemed to stalk her every time she stepped out of her house alone. She was more certain than ever that it was not paranoia. This creepy feeling denoted something as real as the rain falling from the sky.

What does one do when one is being followed?

She made even more haste to her destination. A tendril of fear began to curl around her thoughts and began slowing her, dulling her senses until all she could hear was the sound of her heart pounding in her ears. This was no doubt what her stalker wanted; for her to be paralyzed by fear.

With her free hand, she grabbed a chunk of her heavy skirt and began to run, evading walkers as best as she could. She was certain she looked like a madwoman dashing through the street like that.

She ran into someone, a temperamental person it would seem, for he pushed her back instead of steadying her. She quickly took hold of a street lamp post to regain her balance and leaned against it as she turned her head to look for who might be following. As expected, they were out of sight. An elderly woman walked up to her.

"Are you all right, child?"

Libby nodded and released the lamp post. "I am fine," she croaked.

The elderly woman turned to a few onlookers who had gathered. "Just a frightened girl. Nothing to see."

Heeding her, the onlookers returned to their

business and Libby reached to retrieve the umbrella she had dropped when the man pushed her. She felt a hand on her sleeve and quickly looked up, preparing to defend herself.

"Easy there, child! I am not going to harm you. This is my store," the same woman said, pointing at a sweet shop. "You should come inside out of the rain."

Libby straightened and raised her umbrella to shield herself. "Thank you, but I would rather continue on."

The old lady smiled and asked gently. "Not even for some warm tea? You look like you could use it."

That was when she realized she was shaking like a leaf. She was cold and afraid and alone. She nodded. "Actually, I would like that. Thank you."

The nice woman took her by the arm and led her into her shop. The scent of caramelized sugar and sweet treats filled her nose and began to ease her frayed nerves.

"Would you like to take off your cloak?"

Libby nodded and unclasped the fastening. The woman took the cloak from her and hung it on a coat rack by the door. There was a young woman behind a glass counter that showcased a variety of sweets and chocolate. She gave Libby a nod of acknowledgment and a shy smile.

"Do come through, please," the elderly woman said and led Libby to a small sitting room at the back of the shop. A fire was burning in a small fireplace, the flames radiating warmth and welcome throughout the small space.

"I come back here to rest when there are not many customers around," she supplied as she directed Libby to a chair near the fire. "I can't seem to stand very long these days. Old age." She poked the fire a bit and left the room, presumably to arrange for tea.

Libby looked around, still anxious. The sitting room was very modest and nicely decorated in shades of pale blue and rose. The quality of the furniture was quite good, albeit worn. It was as homely as the owner. She felt herself begin to relax. Not all strangers were bad and perhaps this woman might help her.

A short while later, she returned with a tea tray and set it on a small table between the chairs in front of the fire before pouring and handing her a steaming cup.

"Thank you." Libby accepted it gratefully. Her hand shook when she did.

"Good heavens! You must have had quite the fright. You are still trembling."

Libby tried to smile.

"What is your name, child?"

"Elizabeth," she said without thinking, then checked herself and ensured she did not give her last name.

The woman brightened immediately. "My name is Elizabeth, too!" She clapped her hands together in delight. "I am Mrs. Elizabeth Dawson."

Libby smiled properly at last, feeling more at ease. The warm tea was helping a great deal. She did not know what had come over her but she could remember the fear that had gripped her vividly.

"Pardon my question, but are you in mourning?" the woman asked.

Libby started to shake her head but changed her mind and nodded instead. How else could she explain her attire?

"Husband," she said to a waiting Mrs. Dawson.

"I am so sorry for your loss."

I'm not, she was tempted to say. But she guessed Mrs. Dawson would think her deranged, or worse, heartless.

"You have a nice shop," Libby said, to change the subject.

A proud smile uncreased Mrs. Dawson's features. "It was my father's and he left it for me. In his time, we only sold dry fruits and sugar plums, but when I took over, I expanded it and brought chocolate and other kinds of confectionaries. The caramel is a favorite around here."

Libby was impressed by the woman. It was only a candy store, but she had turned it into something special.

"What brings a genteel lady like you to Roxbury?" When Libby gave her a surprised look, she added, "That is a very fine dress you have on... especially for a widow."

Libby felt somewhat embarrassed by the woman's observation.

"Oh, don't be ashamed of your fortunes, child. I spoil myself too, even at my age. There is a fine French brandy I like to get from my neighbor, Mr. Read..."

The rest of what Mrs. Dawson said faded. Only *Mr. Read* still rang in her head.

"Terrance Read?" she blurted out, and Mrs. Dawson frowned a little as she inclined her head in question.

"Yes. Do you know him?"

"I-I..."

Oh, what was the point of keeping her quest a secret? She was already a murder suspect and the worst that could happen at this point was for her to be killed.

"He is the reason I came to Roxbury. I am in a

spot of trouble and I need information from him that might help me."

"Goodness! Fate works in mysterious ways. He is a good friend of mine." Mrs. Dawson set her empty cup back on the tray and Libby did the same. "Are you acquainted with him then?"

"No. A friend of mine directed me here."

"Would you like me to take you to meet him? Perhaps he will be more forthcoming if he sees us together. He is quite a distrusting man."

For the first time that day, hope shimmered within Libby and she was grateful Mrs. Dawson had found her.

"I would really appreciate that, Mrs. Dawson."

The rain had subsided by now and together, they stepped out of the shop and into Terrance Read's premises.

It was like what she could only describe to herself as an "everything" shop. It sold many things, from fabric, to books to liquor and more. The space was large, too. A gray-haired man looked up from behind a counter and beamed at them, although Libby suspected the welcoming smile was more for Mrs. Dawson than her.

"Elizabeth," he said, walking around the counter to meet them halfway. He kissed both of

Mrs. Dawson's cheeks before looking at Libby with a question in his wary brown eyes.

"Terrance, this is Elizabeth, a friend of mine," she introduced.

He smiled. "Nice to meet you, Miss——"

"Mrs.," Mrs. Dawson corrected.

"My apologies, Mrs...."

"Armstrong," Libby supplied.

Mrs. Dawson took charge and began to explain. "Elizabeth here finds herself in a bit of a mire and she needs your help."

Terrance Read looked around the shop and said in almost a whisper, "We should speak in my office."

He showed them through a door on the right and into his office where they sat in the two chairs in front of a nice oak desk. "I will be right back. I just have to settle the customers in the store."

Mrs. Dawson, after reading the worry in Libby's eyes correctly, reached over and gave her hand a motherly pat. "He will help you if he can. I am sure of it."

Libby returned her smile and tried to relax.

Several minutes later, Mr. Read re-entered the office and sat behind the desk. "How may I help you, Mrs. Armstrong?"

Libby decided to tell him a part of her story,

leaving out details that were not pertinent to the information she needed. "There was a man, Nolan Anthony Hart. He is dead and I am suspected of his murder." She paused there to allow him to react to her revelation. His eyes flared with recognition while beside her, Mrs. Dawson gasped.

"*You* are the one accused of Mr. Hart's murder?" He looked very surprised.

"The police can be quite hopeless sometimes," she replied, trying to insert some levity into her tone.

"But that is impossible. You couldn't have done it."

"That is why I am here, Mr. Read. Lady Sarah Smith-Jones is a very good friend, and I approached her to see what information I might learn. She mentioned that a hit had been put out on the dead man by the Raven, and that she had heard that piece of information from yourself."

His head bobbed. "That is correct."

"May I ask your source? My investigation has revealed that the Raven is actually not responsible. Which means there must be someone spreading this tale around, and I would like to know who."

Mr. Read tapped his teeth while he thought. "I'm sure I got the word from a bartender nearby. Lewis is his name, and his bar is just a block from here if you turn right as you leave. It was also the last place Mr. Hart was seen before he was murdered."

"And do you know where he could possibly have heard that rumor?"

Terrance Read shook his head. "I am afraid I do not know."

"That is all right. I will speak with him."

"He doesn't open until five in the afternoon," he supplied. "It's also…a little rough."

"I can look after myself," she said, with more conviction than she actually felt. She glanced at a clock on the desk. Four hours until the bar opened. "I will be back later." She gave Terrance Read a grateful smile. "Thank you, Mr. Read."

"You should come and taste some of my caramel," Mrs. Dawson said, when they were outside Terrance Read's shop.

Libby followed her back into the sweet shop where she was offered a square piece of caramel with a sprinkling of salt on top, and chocolate. Both were rich in flavor and Libby decided she would make this her favorite sweet shop.

She was still relishing her samples when a bag of sweets was thrust into her hands.

"You can have these for the road," Mrs. Dawson said, grinning at her.

"Oh, you're so very kind," she said, feeling touched by the woman's compassion. "How can I ever repay you?" She was not talking about the sweets, and Mrs. Dawson seemed to understand that.

"You remind me of my daughter, bless her soul. If she had lived, she would have been about your age." She smiled sadly. "If a stranger had helped her, she might still have been here today."

Libby's heart broke. Without thinking, she pulled Mrs. Dawson into a hug. "I will never forget this," she whispered.

She left the shop feeling a hundred times better than when she had entered.

And then she collided with Henry.

CHAPTER TEN

*H*enry had not even considered allowing Libby to come with him to this neighborhood, even though this was the better part of Roxbury. It was not a place for a genteel lady like her. Yes, she was no delicate flower, but she was very vulnerable right now, particularly with someone following her. He had not been able to determine whether they were male or female, for all he had seen the other day was a hooded figure; a dark medieval-style cloak.

His concern for her safety had greatly increased in the past days, as had another feeling he would not dare pause to name.

So, he had come here to Roxbury in his own carriage, to study the murder scene. Without her.

The alley where the murder had allegedly

happened was his first stop. It had not yet been searched by the police. Many days had passed since Mr. Hart's murder and all evidence had most likely been tampered with, but if there truly was something to find, he would find it.

At first, it looked like any alley, in need of some cheer and cleaning, but as he advanced farther in, he found a large brick lying beside the steps to a shop. He put down his bag and picked up the brick to examine. The rain had washed the top surface clean, but when he turned it, he found a crack with a few strands of blonde hair stuck beneath, and a greasy substance that smelled like a cross between perfume and men's cologne. It was a very distinctive odor. He placed the brick back onto the ground before reaching into his bag and retrieving a wooden box. He had several such boxes, ideal for collecting evidence.

Very carefully, he removed a couple of the hairs stuck in the brick's crack and placed it in the box, together with a scraping of the perfumed grease. Mr. Hart had blonde hair, and Mr. Burris had described a distinctive pomade found during the autopsy. And a *boulder* had supposedly been used to bash him on the head. Even though this was not a boulder, it looked sturdy enough to fracture a grown man's skull. He contemplated taking the brick with him, but there was no space for it in his bag, and he couldn't possibly carry it around.

The police could always come back here. If they cared to, that is.

Henry studied the whole area, even in corners looking for more evidence, but he was not as lucky as he'd earlier been. When he was sure there was nothing more for him to find, he picked up his bag and returned to the main street, then continued down.

He spotted a slight woman in a fine black dress that looked uncannily like Libby stepping out of a sweet shop. It couldn't be her, surely? He quickened his pace. The woman turned back to say something to an elderly lady in the shop doorway. When she swiveled to face the street, they collided.

Annoyance filled him. It was, indeed, Libby. What the devil was she doing here in Roxbury? Instead of steadying her, he stepped back. He was too angry with her right now.

"Henry!" she squealed.

"Baroness," he said coolly.

A sheepish smile lit up her face and she held out the paper bag.

"Would you like a sweet?"

"No, thank you."

"All right," she said awkwardly. "It's been nice

running into you...so...I'll be on my way now."
She tried to move past him and he grabbed at
her arm.

"*I'll* take you home. Now." His voice was low
and steely.

She stiffened, clearly receiving the message that
he would brook no argument. He clasped her hand
tightly in his before dragging her down the street in
the direction he had come from. His man and
carriage were waiting where he'd left them, and he
quietly handed her in before joining her.

"Henry," she began nervously.

He did not respond. He could not remember
the last time he had been this angry. It was better to
remain quiet until his ire had abated.

She spoke again. "I—"

He held up a hand to silence her. "Not now,
Libby."

She huffed and turned her face toward the
window. She was sitting on the rear-facing seat and
he was opposite.

Henry thought to wait until they arrived at
Armstrong-Leeds House to censure Libby, but once
he felt calm enough, he spoke. "What were you
doing there?"

She turned her hazel eyes to him and as much
as she made an effort to hide it, there was a

vulnerability there that made him feel churlish for reacting in the way he had.

"I spoke to my friend as I told you I would, and they provided information that led me here." Her voice was solemn.

Now for the real question. "Why didn't you tell *me*?"

Her eyes suddenly flashed with defiance. "I don't remember needing your permission to do anything."

"I am not talking about permission here, and you know it, Libby." His voice rose, together with the anger he had been trying for the past several minutes to tamp down. "This place is *not* an area suitable for a lady—"

"Oh, quit patronizing me! I am more capable than you think. And stop using my class to mask your prejudice."

"I have sisters and I would never allow them to visit places like this."

"Well, I am *not* your sister and I will not have you control my life."

He released an exasperated sigh. One of them had to calm down before they set the carriage on fire, so to speak, and she did not show any sign of coming down from her mantle of ire. He wanted to growl. Instead, he lowered his voice and took slow breaths to regain his composure.

"Libby," he said eventually, in a calmer tone. "I am not controlling your life nor do I wish to do such a thing. I am angry because I was scared for you. This is coming from a place of care and concern."

She continued to glare daggers at him. Clearly, she did not believe him.

"The murder happened not far from where I bumped into you."

Her hand crept up to cover her mouth.

"You, of all people, are especially vulnerable." As her brows came together, he quickly held up a hand. "Don't get me wrong again. I say that, because you are wanted for murder and someone is determined to prove you guilty regardless of the truth. The danger for you is greater than most." Not to mention someone following her. He left that part out so as not to scare her more. He wanted her to be cautious, not terrified.

Her shoulders slumped and she lowered her eyes but not before he caught a glimpse of her inner pain.

He leaned forward and took both of her hands in his. "Forgive me."

"I *am* cautious, Henry," she said, raising her

unguarded eyes to him. "Well, mostly. In this instance, I felt time was not on my side. The sooner I find out the truth the sooner my family will be free." She pulled her hands away and reached into her dress pocket where she brought out a small sheathed dagger. "See? I can defend myself." She returned the dagger and began to reach under her skirt.

His hands shot out instantly to stay her.

"What the devil are you doing?" His voice thickened with both consternation and unexpected desire.

She pushed him away and continued what she was doing and he was torn between curiosity and modesty until she produced a pistol.

Henry's eyes widened. He had thought she could not surprise him more.

"I am a good shot. We can go outside of town if you would like proof."

He closed his mouth which had been hanging open and blinked a few times. He tried to speak, but no sound came out. She had rendered him quite positively speechless.

"So?" she asked, holding the pistol out toward him.

He cleared his throat to find his voice. "Where did you learn to shoot?"

"I practised a lot with Lady Anna growing up,

here and in England, much to our parents' chagrin. When they realized that we could hurt ourselves if left to our supposed vices, they engaged a tutor."

She smiled mischievously and something kicked hard in his chest. God, she was a remarkable woman!

"He only lasted a week," Libby admitted. "Once Anna and I had grasped the basics, we dismissed him."

"I must admit, I am very surprised...and impressed."

Her pretty eyes widened. "You are impressed?" she echoed.

He nodded.

"Every man who has heard that story either cringes, says something I don't like, or challenges me to a competition. And the women," she scoffed. "Well. The women say I am not truly one of them."

Thank the Lord she was not like other women. If he moved in society and was inclined to take a wife, he would have swept Libby away a long time ago.

"It is a foolish society, Libby. Rest assured you will get no such comments from me. As a matter of fact, I dislike shooting at bottles just to prove who is a better shot."

She smiled then. "You and I will get along fine,

then." She raised a cautionary finger. "As long as you trust me and allow me to do what I need to do to clear my name."

"I will allow you that, but only if we work together. As partners."

Her face took on an amused expression. "I agree. Perhaps we will make more headway, working together."

He held out his hand to seal their agreement and she shook it. Just as he had done earlier that morning, he kept her hand in his and she made no move to free herself. When he looked into her eyes, he found a reflection of his own feelings there; the magnetism between them, their matched stubbornness and a strange confusion as to how to behave around the other.

He shook his head, pulling himself out of his daze. He could not be distracted by a beautiful woman and his growing feelings for her at this moment. His focus instead should be helping her to solve the case, and most importantly, keeping her out of trouble.

"I have some news," he said, to shift the mood. "But we will talk about it when I get you home."

Libby finally pulled her hands from his and leaned back in her seat. "I have something to share, too."

He smiled. "It appears we may have both made progress."

"Indeed." She pulled off one of her leather gloves before reaching into the paper bag and pulling out a caramel. She plopped it into her mouth, and chewed daintily. Eventually, she held out the bag to him.

"Are you one of those sticklers who claim sweets rot your teeth?"

"On the contrary." He accepted the bag and looked at the contents. Sugar plums, chocolate, and caramel, his favorite, "I have quite the sweet tooth." Unlike her, he bit his caramel in half, rolling it around in his mouth, savoring the taste before chewing. "And I know an excellent dentist in South End should my teeth get into any trouble."

She laughed softly. "I doubt they will. You have fine teeth."

Heat rose up his cheeks, astonishing him. The last time he had felt near blushing had been in his school days. Libby was fast turning him into a fool and he didn't know what to do to stop it.

"Is that a compliment, Libby?" Henry asked in that baritone that always awakened her awareness.

She felt the heat begin to rise from her neck and knew immediately that she should not have complimented him. But it had not been intentional. It had just popped out of its own accord.

She glanced out the window before replying. They were nearing home. "I don't think it is."

"But I didn't detect any insult there either," he said.

She tried to appear insouciant when she said, "Make of it what you will."

"Oh, I already have." He bowed his head slightly. "And thank you. Compliments don't come my way often."

She gave him a look. "I find that rather hard to believe."

He was a very handsome man and if he moved in society, girls would have thrown themselves at him. Even Libby might have taken a second look--

She quickly shook her head to dismiss the thought.

"It is the truth. I don't exactly have a social circle." He ate another caramel. His fifth one. His comment about having a sweet tooth was true.

"Is that by choice?" she asked. She vaguely knew his family and had met one of his sisters, but knew very little about this man and why he had chosen this life over the one that had been handed to him by birth.

He finished his caramel before replying. "Certainly. I like my life better this way."

"Why *did* you choose to become a private detective?"

He frowned, staring into the sweets bag for an interminable moment. Libby was starting to think that she may have crossed an invisible boundary when he replied.

"I did not feel like I had a purpose. The only communication I had with my father was regarding estate affairs, and my mother…I hardly ever saw her because she was always in her chambers. She was always melancholy. I had little tolerance for the shallowness of society and my friends were few and far between. I felt as though I was not truly living." His silver eyes met hers and he smiled ruefully. "I decided to leave that life behind, and rented apartments in South End."

She found herself smiling, too.

"I remember my first case. I read about a theft in the newspaper and started going around the city investigating, introducing myself as Detective DeHavillend. I caught the thief within two days. It felt…" He paused, then said, "Fulfilling. For the first time. After a few more solo cases, the police took notice and actually approached me to join them. I declined, of course."

"Why?"

"Some of them are very good people, but not all. Others are corrupt and do not truly help those who need it. Many cases go unsolved because of a fear of confronting the members of high society."

"But they are confronting me," she argued.

"Yes, but they are unlikely to convict you, even if you are found guilty. It may well all end up hidden under a rug, so to speak."

That revelation instantly turned Libby's mood sour.

"But then the truth would never come out. What sort of cruelty is that?" She was outraged. She would not be punished for her supposed crime, but her reputation—and that of her family—would remain in tatters. She was paying a price either way, for something that was not her fault.

She closed her eyes and leaned back in her seat.

"I'm sorry for your situation," he said quietly. "I want to make things right."

"Thank you, Henry...for everything." She opened her eyes and stared at him. "You didn't have to help me, but you did."

He took her hands again. "I can't live with

myself if this ruins your life. There must be something I can do to change things."

His words curled around her and that fire that had begun in the center of her heart burned bigger and brighter. It was so short a time to feel this way. Perhaps some of what she was feeling was fueled by gratitude, but it was more than that. Libby understood exactly what was happening to her, and if she had met Henry under different circumstances, things may have been able to play out differently. But she was now a ruined woman, with grime that stained her life. No one would want her.

Days ago, she would have been fine with that idea, but now she had met Henry, and things had changed. *She* had changed.

Something warm touched her cheek and trickled down. Her ungloved hand went up to her face and to her mortification, discovered tears. Even more embarrassing was the fact that she seemed unable to stop them.

Large strong arms came about her and she was pulled across into a warm embrace. "You don't have to be brave, Libby," he said in a soothing tone. "Just be true. Let it out."

As though his words were a command, her body

began to shake and violent sobs wracked her. Her fears and worries all came pouring out.

He held her tighter, speaking words of comfort. Words she heard but didn't process. Everything was blocked out by her grief.

When her sobs finally eased, she snuggled close to Henry. He must think her dramatic right now. But she didn't pull away.

"I am sorry," she sniffled.

He handed her a crisp handkerchief. "Don't ever apologize for something natural." He tucked a finger under her chin and lifted her face, then proceeded to take the handkerchief he'd just given her and began wiping away her tears. "You must have held them in for quite some time, hmm?"

She attempted to smile but more tears escaped, undoing his work. He smiled gently and brushed away a lock of hair that had fallen over her eye.

The carriage slowed, alerting them of their arrival. Unexpectedly, Henry pressed his lips to her forehead and lingered. Libby only then understood that she had been longing for such tenderness for quite some time.

"Come," he said, exiting the carriage first and handing her down before retrieving his bag and giving instructions to his driver. Tucking her hand into the crook of his elbow, they walked up the stairs to Armstrong-Leeds House. Again, she was moved by the attention he was providing. She had, of course, received such attention from him before, but that had merely been chivalry. This was care.

And it endeared him to her all the more.

"I'll go freshen up and perhaps Antoine will show you to the drawing room," she said.

He nodded, staring straight ahead with a frown on his face. She followed his line of sight and her gaze landed on Penforth standing at the top of the stairs.

He was staring straight at them, clearly enraged.

CHAPTER ELEVEN

*P*en's glare was not directed at her—at least not yet—but at Henry. Libby removed herself from his side and went to her brother to try and placate him. Pen was an irascible man and he could very well start a fight with Henry if he thought she had been in any physical or moral danger.

It was paramount that she doused the flame before it turned into a conflagration.

"Pen—"

"You fool!" He pushed Libby out of the way and advanced toward Henry.

She jumped to insert herself between them, placing her hands on Pen's chest to stop him. "It is not his fault," she said firmly, holding his dark gaze.

"I went out by myself and Henry found me. He was looking out for me, Pen."

"That so?" He stared at Henry.

"Yes," Henry replied.

"Let's go inside. We need to talk." Pen took hold of her arm. "You too, detective," he said to Henry over his shoulder.

Libby wrenched her arm free. "I will not be treated like a child. I am a grown woman and the decision to leave the house was entirely mine. I will go inside, but you will not drag me."

Her brother's eyes flared momentarily, but then he relented and waved for her to precede him.

When she entered, Anna was standing anxiously at the foot of the stairs, looking apologetically at Libby.

"I am sorry," she mouthed.

Libby shook her head as she crossed the hall to the drawing room. "It is not your doing, Anna."

Penforth walked in with Henry behind him. He appeared unperturbed by Pen's anger.

"Will you tell me what you were doing out of the house?" Pen asked, crossing his arms over his chest.

"I don't remember ever needing your permission before leaving the house." She tossed the bag of remaining sweets onto the side table, and matched his stance by folding her arms across her own bosom.

"That was before the incident," her brother argued, his voice increasing tempo. "Anything could have happened to you."

"NOT THIS AGAIN!" LIBBY STAMPED HER FOOT, AND Henry felt his brows rise. "I am sick of everyone trying to tell me what to do and what not to do. I am aware of the dangers out there. *Devil take it*, I have survived one of them!"

Sir Penforth clamped his mouth shut and stared at her, visibly shocked at her outburst. Henry was surprised too. She could move in and out of moods very fast. Just moments ago, she was broken and in tears. Now, she was practically setting the drawing room on fire.

"The police want me for murder, Pen, and I will not sit in my room and let my life be decided by someone else. I am not guilty and I will find the truth. So, before you start getting angry next time, think of my motives for going out."

"Well, there you have it," Henry said, almost laughing at the antics of brother and sister.

The man ignored his quip. "Forgive me, Libby. I

should have paid more attention to how you were feeling."

She sighed and lowered herself onto the sofa.

"Sir Penforth," Henry began. "Libby and I—"

"Libby?" Sir Penforth's expression turned wild again. "You use her Christian name?"

"Oh, for heaven's sake, Penforth!" Libby shot back to her feet. "If you so desperately need to fight someone, there are bars and clubs for you to visit. Henry has not wronged you in any way." She stepped closer to her brother. "Nor me. Yes, we are informal with each other. If you have a problem with it, go vent to Anna."

A stifled laugh came from behind Henry, and he turned to find Duchess Wrexford holding her hands over her mouth. That drew Sir Penforth's attention away from him. His expression softened a touch and Henry realized there must be romance between them.

He usually checked the backgrounds of the people he worked with, but this case had been a most unusual one right from the start, and it had skipped his mind. He did not know very much about Libby's family, other than what was in the public eye. He was aware that her brother and the duchess had led her rescue when she had been kidnapped, but that was where his knowledge ended.

"This is all very unnecessary, Pen, don't you think?" Lady Anna said, walking up to Libby and taking her arm. "Come, Libby, let's give them a moment to speak as men. If they want to brawl it out, I say we let them."

Libby allowed her friend to lead her out of the room. Sir Penforth's eyes were still on Lady Anna, and the choler radiating from him had decreased considerably.

"Just don't lose a tooth before our wedding," the duchess called over her shoulder from the doorway. "I will be most vexed."

Ah, so they were even engaged to be married. It seemed there had been no formal announcement yet.

Sir Penforth's lips curved very lightly at her words. The woman obviously had a positive influence on him and that was certainly an achievement on her part. The man was usually like stone, unfeeling and unrelenting.

Henry wondered if a woman would ever have a similar influence on him; if her presence could alleviate his anger and her words bring him comfort. Libby immediately popped into his head. He had never thought about the pursuit of romance. He had been far too busy.

But now that he had met Libby, thoughts of romance and even love, had been stirring in his mind. No matter how many times he dismissed the thoughts as frivolous, they always came back, especially when he least expected them.

Like now.

What did this mean?

"Please, have a seat." Sir Penforth's voice broke the line of his thoughts.

Henry blinked. All that hostility that had been oozing from him was no more. He even said *please* without being derisively mocking.

He sat and Sir Penforth did the same.

"I lashed out because of concern for my sister," he said. "She is going through so much and I don't want her suffering more."

"I don't, either," Henry responded.

"What is happening? I need you to be completely honest with me."

"I certainly have no other choice," he jested. "I don't know what the Duchess would do to me if I knock out your teeth."

Sir Penforth did not appear to be amused by the statement.

"I have been investigating on my own. Perhaps I should have informed you…" Henry frowned and corrected himself. "I *should* have informed you. She is your sister and you personally approached me to take on the case. I beg your pardon."

Sir Penforth nodded. Henry had half expected him to react negatively.

"At the same time, Libby——" The man gave him a warning look. Henry did not care and continued. "Libby was also investigating. When I found out, we decided to work together."

Sir Penforth sighed heavily. "She and Anna will be the death of me." He shook his head. "What progress have you made?" He had most likely realized the futility of trying to oppose them.

"She is definitely being framed. Someone—most likely the killer—is trying to convince everyone that she did it. I went down to Roxbury, to assess the murder scene, and found some evidence which I am going to take to the police when I leave here."

"What kind of evidence?"

"Strands of hair that look like those of the deceased."

"How will that help Libby?"

"It may not help a lot right now, but I want to study the hair a little more closely in conjunction with the body. I believe I found the site of the murder today, and the murder weapon."

Penforth nodded in comprehension.

"Libby," Henry started, and found he quite enjoyed taunting Sir Penforth by using her name. "Libby, on the other hand, has made much more progress than I have. There is a rumor that a hit was placed on Mr. Hart by a man called the Raven."

"I know him," Penforth said. "Owner of The Barbican. His real name is Tamworth Arbusson. Bastard son of a duke. He is a very intelligent and dangerous man, but I can't see him doing something like that. At least, he would not have it done in such a sloppy manner."

"Precisely," Henry agreed, admiring the man's perception. "Libby and I visited with him and he denies any and all involvement. I believe him, given the deceased owed him a great deal of money. What use would a dead man be, in repaying a debt?"

Penforth looked thoughtful.

"Then I found out this morning during my visit to the police station that a witness came forward. She—"

"*She?*"

"Yes, it is a woman—a high-born lady, apparently—but unfortunately I do not know who she is as the police are keeping that information from me."

Penforth cursed under his breath.

"She claimed that she saw a woman fitting Libby's description kill Mr. Hart in an alley in Roxbury. The same place I found the murder weapon. Now, I don't believe your sister did it. I am well past that point. Someone is trying to pin it on her—and perhaps using the Raven as a back-up plan. I think if we can find out who is spreading the rumors, it might lead us to the real killer."

"Good work, DeHavillend." Henry felt unaccountably pleased at the praise.

The other man then inclined his head in a questioning manner. "You did all of this without a contract in place. Why?"

Henry shrugged. "She needs my help."

"You didn't start looking for Lady Kingsleigh's necklace until a contract was in place."

"I see you have been researching me," Henry intoned. "Lady Kingsleigh is not an innocent woman with a ruined reputation. I only took that case to pass time."

"Would you like a contact drawn now?" Penforth asked coolly.

Did Henry want to be paid for this?

"No, that will not be necessary."

Penforth's eyes narrowed with suspicion.

"You and I both know you are not a charity

worker, DeHavillend. What do you stand to gain from this?"

"What if I told you that I am not looking to gain anything? Would you believe me?"

Libby's brother shook his head slowly. "No, I would not." After a moment of silence, he mused, "Perhaps it is her affection you are after?"

Henry did not respond, but he felt his cheeks heat up. He was saved from a speculative look from Penforth when Libby and Duchess Wrexford returned. Both men rose as the ladies walked in. Libby had changed into a different dress. She looked fresh and very attractive indeed.

"Good to see the two of you have not killed each other," she said.

"We should eat," Libby said, looking pointedly at Henry. "I am sure you are hungry. I know I am."

He grinned. "Certainly."

In the dining room, he met Lady Christiana Armstrong-Leeds, a beautiful, albeit frail-looking, woman. He now knew where Libby got her looks, and yet the two women were as different as could be. Sixteen-year-old Lady Mary was also introduced to him; a sweet girl with a calm disposition that girls her age sorely lacked.

"I have heard quite a bit about you and your detective work, my Lord," Libby's mother said.

"There is not another private detective as good as you in Boston, they say. How true is that?"

Hmm. So, Lady Christiana was not as docile as he thought. She was already interviewing him.

His food was served just then; a creamy soup with chicken and vegetables, cold meats, cheese, and bread. His lunch usually was whatever he could scrounge at that moment. It could be anything from a pie to a bowl of soup.

But this...

Eating together with people was something he had not experienced in a very long time, not even when he still lived with his family. It evoked a strange sense of longing within him.

"Detective?"

He looked up to find everyone waiting for his response to Libby's mother.

"Pardon me, my lady. I may have gotten lost wool gathering."

She smiled coolly at him and he realized he should be addressing her question and not excusing his momentary lapse in attention. He cleared his throat. "I simply like what I do, and perhaps that leads me to do it well."

She smiled, this time with more emotion on her fine face. "I quite like you, my Lord. You should come by more frequently."

He bowed his head slightly in courtesy. "I shall try, my lady."

"What made you decide to take on this case after rejecting it the first time?"

This was not a question Henry wanted to answer now, especially when his stomach needed tending to.

But did he have a choice?

He glanced at Libby and found her lost in her food, oblivious to her mother's interrogation. But she could very well be paying attention and not show it.

"It is merely a change of heart. I had reservations and they were settled quickly."

She pursed her lips as if she was giving what he had just said some serious thought. He used the time to eat and was halfway through his soup when she spoke again.

"My Lord, why did you choose this life?"

The same question Libby had asked. Henry almost choked on his soup.

CHAPTER TWELVE

"Should you really be asking him that, Mama?" Libby stepped in, and he smiled inside.

He had been right about her paying attention and not showing it.

"I don't know of a better time to ask," Lady Christiana said baldly. "What if he finds this family too odd and never returns after his business with us is concluded? When will I ever get the chance to sate my curiosity?"

He liked Lady Christiana, he decided. She was bold in her own way.

Libby shrugged and continued eating, seemingly satisfied with her mother's answer. She was not seeking to impress him and he liked that about her.

He turned back to the older woman. "I wanted

excitement. And purpose," he answered simply and her eyes widened a little.

"There is quite some excitement to be had in life, without putting yourself in harm's way."

"My work is quite safe," he assured her.

"How many murder cases have you successfully solved?" This question was from Libby's sister, and it caught him off guard.

"That's quite enough, Mary. This is not suitable discussion for the dinner table," Pen said, and a chorus of female laughter broke out around the table.

My, but this was an unusual group of people. Henry's grin grew wide. What he found most endearing was their informality. He had assumed them to be like any other elite Boston society family. Stiff and proper; a mirror of his own family. But they were clearly modern in their outlook; far more accepting of female independence than was standard. Their coming together for lunch was telling of their closeness as a family. His family rarely dined together, most preferring to have their food taken up to their chambers.

When he looked up, he found Libby's amber gaze on him, curious and piercing, and he wondered if she had any clue that he was growing to envy the richness of her life.

"It has been pleasant dining with you, my Lord," Lady Christiana said when they finished. "I know you have a lot to do so I will not bother you now, but I would like to invite you to dinner with us tomorrow evening if you are free?"

When was the last time he had received a proper dinner invitation?

"I would be delighted." He bowed.

Libby came up beside him and took his arm, leading him from the dining room to the salon. The place he'd seen her for the first time. So much had happened between then and now.

"Shall we get back to work?" she asked, sitting on a green damask sofa.

"Will your brother and Lady Anna be joining us?"

"No. Unless you want them to be here?"

"I prefer it just the two of us," he admitted.

Libby smiled. "Good. So do I."

That smile...it was not the widest he'd seen, but it affected him as though it were.

"There is a man named Terrance Read," Libby said, drawing his attention back to business. "He owns a shop in Roxbury and it was he who told my friend of the rumor. I met him today and he pointed me to a bar. The bartender, a man named Lewis, is his source. I don't know his last name."

She frowned. "I am not sure why I did not ask for it. But I know where the bar is. It opens at five every afternoon. I thought perhaps we could return, together."

His heart beat faster. A proper lead at last. "Yes, we certainly should. Perhaps his information will give us more material that I can take to the police."

She nodded contemplatively. "I'll get my cloak."

"Are you not going to wear your black dress?" he teased.

She made a face. "It needs to be cleaned. Besides, I don't think I want to be wearing it anymore. I don't need to hide."

He studied her face. She was definitely confident. "What brought on that realization?"

"Being caught by you, believe it or not." An embarrassed smile curved her soft lips. "I should get my cloak."

"Of course."

Moments after Libby left him, Lady Mary walked in with a brown cat dogging her steps.

"Detective." She inclined her head in greeting.

He rose to his feet and smiled down at her.

"This is my cat, Treacle," she introduced. "He has quite the attitude, but once he is familiar with you, you will find him very sweet."

Just then, the cat rubbed itself against Henry's legs and looked up at him, purring.

"Oh, he already likes you!"

Henry grinned. "Was that a test, Lady Mary?"

She sat on the sofa opposite him and Treacle jumped onto her lap. "Perhaps. But it is not for you. It is for Treacle. You see, we once had a maid and he never liked her. Whenever he saw her, he hissed. One day, the maid was caught searching Libby's room for something. She was dismissed immediately but we never got to figure out what she had been looking for and why."

"Ah, so you believe the cat can sense dishonest people?"

She stroked Treacle's fur. "Maybe. And maybe it is just a coincidence."

"I have heard some animals have stronger senses than ours so it could be possible. A feline, after all, is a hunter. Even a domesticated one."

She was studying him and he was uncertain why. Much like Libby, Mary was obviously a very curious soul and he could sense a hankering for adventure in her.

"How many murder cases have you successfully solved, Detective?"

Henry chuckled. "You have not forgotten about your question."

"You owe me an answer."

"I have been a detective for five years and I have successfully solved seven murder cases in that time," he replied.

Henry's career in crime-solving had begun when he was twenty-seven and he had come a long way since then. He was proud of himself and what he had achieved.

"That *is* impressive!" Her dark eyes gleamed with curiosity and excitement. "Do you think I could do that too?"

Ah, there it was! Her reason for asking all those questions.

"Or are you like most men who think it is not appropriate for a woman to solve crimes?"

He answered truthfully. "Libby is helping me solve her own case, and she is doing even better than I am. I don't see any reason why a woman should not solve crimes. You are every bit as capable as a man. Perhaps even better."

"Will you coach me?"

He had been wanting to hire an assistant, most likely an apprentice, and Lady Mary was giving him the opportunity to select her. He chuckled, thinking of what society would say of a genteel lady becoming a detective.

It was brilliant!

"If you obtain your mother and brother's permission, we can discuss it further."

She leapt from her chair, scaring the cat who had begun sleeping. It yelped and ran out of the room. "Thank you, Detective! Oh, thank you!"

The sound of a throat being cleared had both of them turning toward the doorway. Libby stood there, with her cloak, gloves and hat, ready to go.

"Detective DeHavillend has agreed to take me on as an apprentice," Lady Mary announced excitedly.

Libby looked slowly from Henry to her sister, causing nerves to rise.

"I didn't know you wanted to go into crime-solving," she said to her sister.

"I didn't know I wanted to, either. Until you disappeared weeks ago. I was left sitting here at home while Anna and Pen went out to look for you. Libby, I felt so helpless."

Libby's expression turned soft and she went to her sister, taking her hands.

"I want to be able to help people," Lady Mary added, and Libby's eyes misted. They hugged.

Either Henry was becoming emotional, or there was something wrong with him. Being emotional counted as wrong in his experience. Ever since he'd walked into this house today, he had been feeling things, and not just his growing feelings for Libby. He had a yearning for inclusion. He did not realize how starved he had been until now.

His heart twisted and he had to remind himself that he was not a dreamer. He woke every morning and stared reality in the face. Men like him should not reach for things they could not have. It would not end well.

"Shall we?" He held his arm out to Libby. To Libby's sister he said, "Not without your mother and brother's permission, my lady. Remember that."

"Call me Mary, please."

"Then call me Henry."

"See you later, Henry."

LIBBY WAS MOVED BY HENRY'S ACTIONS. SHE HAD heard him telling Mary that women were just as capable of solving crimes as men. Perhaps even better. She was developing respect for him before now, and that stepped things up a notch.

"It was nice what you agreed to do for Mary," she said quietly, once they were in his carriage.

He smiled without saying anything. They sat in comfortable silence for almost half the ride. Libby felt like she had known him for a very long time and appreciated his company. She was not sure if he felt the same, but after seeing how well he fit in at the family lunch, she wanted him to.

She also wanted to be fine if he didn't feel the same. It would be hard to accept, and she wanted to hold onto this moment for as long as she could. Once the case was over, he would be out of her life, and although he might be working with her sister—if Pen would allow it—he would be so busy with work they would likely slip back into being strangers.

It was a painful thought.

But she had to be strong. It was the only way she could get her life back to a semblance of its former state.

"You are very quiet," came his deep voice. It spread through the darkened carriage to reach her. "Is something the matter?"

Yes, there was, but she couldn't tell him.

"I am tired," she lied.

"The excuse every woman gives when she does not want to talk," he drawled.

"And how would you know that?"

"You may be tired, but it never stops you from expressing yourself, Libby."

He was coming to know her rather well. She

remembered when Anna and Pen had come to rescue her from the chapel crypts. The first thing she had said to them was, "Took you long enough," and "Do you know how dark and lonely this place is?"

"You can talk to me, Elizabeth," he prodded, using her full name for once.

That made her smile. "I like being called Libby, but Elizabeth sounds quite nice when you say it."

He grinned rakishly. "Would you like me to continue, then?"

A little laugh escaped. "No, because then it might lose its charm."

"True." He leaned back and regarded her with his electric silver eyes. "You have successfully evaded my question and even changed the subject." She opened her mouth to speak but before she could say anything, he shook his head. "I am not going to push you. If you want to tell me, you will tell me when you are ready."

Libby smiled again. Her heart might be aching, but at least her face was smiling.

"A witness came forward today and gave the police a statement," Henry said at last. "She—"

"She?" Libby interrupted.

"Yes, it was a female, but the police will not

disclose her identity. They keep some things from me in order to try to convince me to join them."

"How very petty. And they are foolish to think withholding information is good leverage with you. You can always find out yourself."

His eyes turned admiring. "Perhaps *you* should join me in crime-solving, too. You have the spirit and intelligence for it."

"You cannot handle Mary and me at the same time," she pointed out.

"You may be right. The two of you might just be the death of me."

Libby got an idea. She could take up crime-solving as a hobby in order to keep him in her life. She saved the idea in a box in her mind to be examined and expanded upon at a later time.

Now, back to the witness.

"What did the witness say?"

"She described a woman like you carrying out the murder…"

Libby felt irritation and anger crawling inside her at the unfairness of everything. Someone was trying very hard to frame her.

"The witness was correct about the crime scene, but the bit about you doing the deed could not be further from the truth."

At least he believed her.

"We need to find this woman, Henry," she said.

"Yes, we do," he agreed as she felt the carriage slow down. "We will get to Lewis first, and then the woman. If he leads us to her, that would be great."

The carriage stopped and they disembarked. The streets of Roxbury were even darker now as the faded light called in the night and Libby was glad Henry was there with her.

But not even his presence could chase away the shadow that crept up on her once more. She felt it again, that ominous presence that had her utterly disoriented earlier. Libby hated to think about what would have happened to her had Mrs. Dawson not come to her rescue.

"Henry," she whispered, "you might think me paranoid, but I feel like we are being followed."

Henry continued walking, looking straight ahead as though he had not heard her. Was she truly imagining things?

"I know," he said at last.

Relief washed through her. "I am not imagining things, then."

"I saw someone following you on two occasions," he said in a very low voice. "But unfortunately, they disappeared before I could identify them. Come." He steered her into the first shop they found. It was a jewelry store with a middle-aged man behind the counter.

When he saw them, he came round to greet them.

"Good evening, Sir, Madam. How may I help you?"

"Err…" Libby began.

Henry took over. "We would like to check your wares, please."

The jeweler's face brightened at the prospect of patronage. Libby felt guilty. They were not here to purchase jewelry. They were hiding from a stalker.

The man moved behind the counter and waved for them to join him. "What would you like?" he asked.

"A ring, for my *fiancée*," Henry supplied, looking down at Libby with a strange little grin.

Are you out of your mind? she wanted to ask.

"Oh, my felicitations, Sir, and you too, Madam."

Libby smiled tautly and pushed her elbow into Henry's ribs. He stiffened for a moment but once he recovered, he circled his arm around her waist and pulled her close. The jeweler gave them a knowing look.

"We are looking for something unique, not the common ring design."

"I have just the thing for you." The jeweler bent and retrieved a folder. He opened it and pointed at the drawing of a ring with a briolette-cut gem.

Libby liked it instantly. If she were to choose a ring for herself, she would go for exactly this. The pear-shaped cut was complex and the shine was sure to be brilliant. But she already had many jewels and was not in need of a new one. Besides, this was an engagement ring and not something she could ever hope for.

"Do you like this one, dear heart?" Henry asked, leaning close.

Libby's cheeks flamed. She was not enjoying this game because it played with her emotions. Couldn't they just leave and head to Lewis's bar?

"Libby," he whispered in her ear. "Discretion is important during investigations. We are posing as an engaged couple and it would do us a world of good if you chose a ring. We will not be buying, obviously, but we will keep suspicion at bay."

He was right. It was a good plan, but she didn't have to like it. The jeweler was a stranger, after all.

"Very well."

She feigned a brilliant smile. "We would like this one." She pointed at the picture of the ring in the folder.

"Excellent choice, Madam. Do you have a gemstone in mind or shall I recommend?"

"Emerald and topaz to match her eyes," Henry said. "They are a delightful combination of green, brown and amber and I doubt any one gem can do them justice."

She didn't quite know how to respond to that.

The jeweler peered at her. "I agree. The primary gem should be topaz and the emeralds can be the surround."

"That sounds perfect," Henry said like a proud fiancé.

"I will show you the stones now, please give me a moment."

"Please take your time," Libby said brightly as he disappeared into the back room. Then she turned to Henry. "I don't like this," she complained.

"I know."

"We could have just pretended we were lost and left."

"Maybe I find playacting fun, Libby."

"I don't find it funny, Henry. This man thinks we are really purchasing a ring from him." She truly was feeling guilty about this.

Henry's hands moved up to her shoulders. "He will make a beautiful ring and if we don't buy it, he will just place it on display." He waved toward a display case on the other side of the room with beautiful jewels inside. "We will not be causing him any loss."

She sighed.

"Listen," he said very gently. "I will return after about a week and tell him you have begged off and we are no longer getting married."

"And paint me black?" she exclaimed.

Henry laughed. The nerve of him! "You will not be painted any color. It is a woman's prerogative to change her mind about the man she is marrying. The main reason I am doing this, Libby, is to keep you safe. We don't know anything about this jeweler and in case he knows something, we get the upper hand by keeping him from suspecting anything."

Oh, Henry. He knew how to make her feel happy and sad at the same time. He was protecting her which equated to happy. But romance was not his intention, despite the picture they were presenting, and that made her sad.

"Fine. Let's get it over with."

He smiled devilishly as the jeweler returned with gemstones on a small silver platter.

"This is a smoky topaz." He held up a yellow-brown gemstone to the light. It sparkled beautifully. "This can represent the amber and brown in your eyes, Madam." He replaced it and picked up an emerald. "This is for the green."

"I like them," she said, meaning her words. "Let's have it made."

The jeweler nodded happily. "Excellent! The ring will be ready in four days."

"Let's discuss price," Henry said.

A figure was quoted—a rather large sum, but the ring was worth it—and Libby couldn't tamp down the guilt that rose.

"I will have a check sent to you," Henry said confidently. "May I have your name, Sir?"

"Edward…Edward Kent."

He fished out a small book from his coat pocket and made a show of taking the details. The unsuspecting jeweler beamed, thanking them for their *wonderful* patronage.

Libby felt like a fraud.

"Don't worry." Henry patted her hand after they had stepped out of the shop. "I will not leave him empty when I return."

That eased her guilt somewhat.

But now they were out on the street once more she was instantly reminded of the stalker.

CHAPTER THIRTEEN

*H*enry surveyed the street for any sign of the person who had been stalking them but found nothing.

"You said you saw them?"

He looked down at Libby's panicked face and his insides twisted. She had known all along that she was being stalked, but had braved it out, thinking she was imagining things. The poor girl.

Henry wanted to pull her into his arms and promise her that no harm would ever come to her. But he did not dare.

"The person was wearing a black medieval-style cloak. I never got close enough to determine if it is a man or a woman, but the height points to a man if that is anything to go by. We should keep a keen eye. Are you still armed?"

She quirked a fine dark brow. "What do you think?"

"Point taken."

They began walking up the street with Libby directing them to Lewis's bar. They had spent more time than they should have in the jewelry store. No matter how fast they worked, they could not find and interrogate Lewis in time to be on their way before the streets were completely deserted. Right now, people were already moving off the streets and out of the cold.

They walked past the sweet shop Libby had exited earlier. Had that been just this afternoon? It felt longer ago than that.

"I met a woman here earlier," Libby said as passed the shop. "Mrs. Dawson. I had something of a panic and she helped me."

Henry stopped short and she almost stumbled from the abrupt change of pace. "What happened?" he asked, alarmed.

"I felt I was being followed and started to run. I bumped into a man and almost fell. Mrs. Dawson found me and took me into her shop where she gave me some tea and warmed me by the fire."

"Holy God, Libby!" He pulled her into his arms.

"I am fine," she mumbled into his coat.

"I know." It was all he could manage for a moment. He was just thankful that no harm had come to her.

"Now, the bar is just ahead," she said. "Shall we get this over with so we can go home?" An impish smile curved her lips and shone in her eyes as she looked up at him.

He sighed, finally releasing her. "Come, then." He took her arm and they continued.

"There," she said, pointing at a sign that read: Lewis's Bar.

Henry didn't like the kind of men he was seeing going into the premises. "Is there no way I can convince you to turn back?"

"We have come too far, Henry."

At the door, he looked down at her. "Libby…"

She shook her head. "If I didn't stop before now, what makes you think I will stop now?"

"I thought I might get lucky."

She tugged at his coat and he led them into the bar.

The smell of cigar smoke and alcohol was the first thing to hit him. He scanned the room casually, taking note of the faces of the men, the setting of the bar. His gaze settled on a man who looked to be about his own age behind the bar counter. There were tall shelves behind him with countless bottles of liquor.

Nothing appeared out of the ordinary.

Then, as he turned to look at Libby, the second thing hit him.

His eyes caught a cloak hanging on the coat hanger next to the door. A black medieval-style cloak. Something heavy sank to the bottom of his stomach as his senses picked up. He drew Libby nearer.

"Let's see if we can find Lewis," he whispered.

On their way to the bar, a man accosted them.

"We don't allow women in here," he said. He was a burly man with bloodshot eyes and bad breath that indicated he'd over-imbibed.

"Is that so?" Henry asked in a casual yet ironic tone.

"Yes," the man said slowly.

"Are you Lewis, the owner of this establishment?" He raised his voice so most of the people around could hear. This man was not Lewis. No barkeeper drank his liquor in excess.

"What does it matter? No women allowed."

"We were passing and suddenly my wife," he glanced down at Libby who was watching everything with a puzzled frown on her face, "developed chills. We need some whiskey or brandy to warm her. She was born with a rare disease that causes her to feel severely cold."

Beside him, he felt Libby begin to shake. Clever girl. He did not look at her so as not to lose his composure.

"I couldn't possibly leave her outside in her condition." He inserted enough emotion into his voice to sound like a distressed husband. He pulled a shaking Libby closer. He was unsure where he was going with this but hoped it would work.

"That's enough, Marcus!" The man behind the counter called out as he walked up to them. "Please forgive me. This fool is always trying to drive my customers away."

"My wife needs help. Is there somewhere private she could rest, so she does not bother your other customers with her presence?"

"Rest assured that this establishment is not a men-only establishment. It is Marcus who makes such ridiculous claims." He rolled his eyes. "Sometimes I wish he was not my brother."

"I think she will still need somewhere private. I will pay you. Handsomely."

People understood the language of money very well, Henry knew. There was hardly an unfavorable situation that money did not turn favorable.

"Follow me, please," the bartender said politely.

Henry and Libby followed him into a room that looked like a storage area with barrels of ale and wine on one side and crates on the other. He nudged Libby to sit on one of the three chairs in the room near the crates before taking another seat himself.

"Will any liquor do or is there a specific one that makes her better?" the barkeeper asked.

"Whiskey will be fine, thank you." He gave the man some money.

When he left to fetch Libby's *medicinal drink*, she stopped shaking and glared at Henry as soon as the door was shut.

"First, I am your fiancée, and now your wife? Were you ever going to ask my consent?"

Oh, he had done badly.

She had played along perfectly but deep inside she must think him the worst sort of cur. She had every right to be angry with him. She had been forced to marry before and would naturally not find this situation amusing, in the least.

"I am sorry, Libby. I was not thinking."

"Well, *think* next time," she snapped. "I will not play such games again."

He hoped there wouldn't be a next time.

"Forgive me."

Footsteps approached and she began to shiver

again. When their eyes met, she shot him another withering glare.

His former self—the man he had been a week ago—would not have been concerned with her feelings and whether or not she was hurt. That was no longer the case.

The bartender opened the door and walked in with an entire bottle of whiskey and two glass tumblers. He placed them on a crate near Henry and made to leave.

"Are you Lewis?" Henry asked.

He turned with his hand on the door handle, looking unsure. "Yes, I am."

"Thank God!" Henry said affectedly. "We need your help."

Lewis released the door handle and moved closer. Henry began pouring a drink for Libby, talking as he did so.

"We were led to you by Mr. Read." Lewis's eyes narrowed just a touch. "I am an investigator and my wife and I work cases together. This particular case is causing her quite a bit of distress, as you can see. We only need information."

He handed Libby a glass and she took a sip. He refrained from pouring some for himself.

Lewis looked at her shivering, and a sympathetic expression replaced the skeptical one.

"Of course, I would like to help if I can. And Mr. Read is a respectable businessman. I trust him."

"We are looking for the source of a rumor about the Raven ordering the murder of Mr. Nolan Hart."

"Ah, I told Mr. Read about that one last week when he stopped by."

"And who did you hear it from?"

"A man came in on the day Mr. Hart's body was found. I heard him telling another man that the Raven ordered it. I overheard the conversation and didn't pay it any mind, but then more people started talking about it."

"Do you know the name of the first man you heard it from?"

"I'm afraid I don't. I didn't see him again, until now."

"Now?"

"Yes, he is in the bar as we speak. You arrived not long after him."

Henry shot to his feet. "Show me, please."

Lewis nodded and opened the door. He stared around the room, with Henry following his line of sight.

"I am sorry," he said. "It appears he has gone."

Henry released a disappointed breath but then remembered something and his eyes went straight to the coat rack by the door. The black cloak was missing. If the cloaked person stalking them was the same as the man spreading the rumors, then they would just have to double their efforts to locate him. At least now they knew it was a man.

"Lewis, did this man wear a black woolen cloak?"

"Yes. Yes, he did. How do—"

"I am a detective." He reached into his pocket and retrieved some money which he offered to the man. "Thank you for your help."

"You don't have to pay me for that. I am happy to help a good cause." Lewis paused then. "You are looking to solve the murder, aren't you?"

Henry nodded.

"Mr. Hart was a menace, but a murder is a murder. We need to feel safe in our neighborhood. I will not accept payment from you, Sir. You are doing a service for us all. As a matter of fact, I wish to return the money you paid for the whiskey."

"That won't be necessary."

"I insist."

"Then you can give some of the customers here a drink on the house."

Lewis smiled. "I will do just that."

He felt Libby come up beside him and instinctively, his hand found hers and held it.

"I feel much better, Lewis, thank you," she said.

The bartender bowed slightly. "It is my pleasure."

"Should we go?" she asked Henry and he nodded.

He went back into the storeroom to retrieve his bag. He was used to this; carrying this bag around with him all over the city.

They left the bar and although the person they were searching for still eluded them, Henry was convinced they were getting closer. The streets were almost deserted and they walked briskly back to his carriage and were soon on their way back to Beacon Hill.

"I heard what Lewis told you," Libby said, sounding tired. "You made mention of a black cloak."

He leaned forward. "The person I saw following you wore a woolen medieval-style cloak with a hood. There was a similar cloak hanging in the bar and Lewis confirmed that he heard the rumor from the cloak's owner."

"And he doesn't know the man's name?"

"Sadly not."

She sat up suddenly as though she was just realizing something. "We are very close, Henry. We only have to find him now. We need to ask around."

"Yes," he agreed. "But I would suggest we return in the daytime."

"Of course." She smiled at him then and he found himself smiling back as the worry tightening his chest began to loosen.

"Libby…I wasn't thinking when I made up—"

She held up a hand to stop him. "It worked and that's what matters. I am just a bit sensitive about it. I was forced to marry a man who abducted me and now, by law, I am a widow."

"I think you are very brave." He took her small gloved hands. "I know of a man who may be able to help expedite the annulment without waiting until the investigation is concluded. I can have him call you if you wish."

Her eyes misted. "You will?"

"Of course." Henry was starting to think he would do anything for her at this point. "He owes me a favor."

"Thank you, Henry," she whispered.

"Think nothing of it."

Libby leaned back and the journey continued on in silence with each of them lost in their thoughts.

They were close to finding the truth. He was certain of it. Henry couldn't be happier but at the same time, a feeling of dread was building. Once the case was solved, he would no longer have a reason to spend time with Libby. Things would go back to the way they were before he knew her, and she would probably marry some wealthy gentleman with a fancy title.

No, no, no. This Libby sitting opposite him would not marry a wealthy gentleman with a fancy title. This Libby might never marry at all. That thought worried him the most.

He looked at her and realized she had fallen asleep.

He moved very carefully from his seat to hers and shifted a lock of hair off her cheek. The street lamps they passed cast a sporadic glow across her delicate features. He committed every feature, every contour of her face to memory, for he may not get such a chance again.

Very slowly, he leaned forward and pressed his lips to her forehead. He would have loved to kiss her on the lips but that would be a liberty too far. He had never been more certain of someone's innocence than right now, and he had never been more determined to discover the truth.

CHAPTER FOURTEEN

*O*n the front steps of Armstrong-Leeds House, Libby invited him to have dinner with her and her family, but he declined politely. "Your mother has already invited me tomorrow."

"That was my mother's invitation. This is mine."

"I need to get home and record our findings, Libby. I will see you on the morrow."

She pouted like a child and he tweaked her nose playfully.

"Aren't you hungry?" she enticed.

Of course, he was, but he had to get back to his place. There was too much swirling around in his mind.

"Good night, Elizabeth," he murmured.

"Good night, Henry."

Instead of stepping down onto the street, he remained looking at her. How foolish he must appear to any passerby that should encounter the scene, but he did not care.

"Come inside," she insisted.

"I should not."

This time, he did try to leave. It was difficult but he managed it in the end, with a rather large and probably silly grin.

The grin did not last long, for he caught sight of a hooded figure in the distance. A medieval cloak! This time, he ran. The cloaked figure began to run too, and Henry moved even faster. He had closed half of the distance between them when the figure turned into an alley. Henry had no choice but to follow.

It was a closed alley but there was no sign of the person he had chased in. Henry started to reach for the pistol in his coat pocket but before he could pull it out, someone grabbed him from behind, pinning his arms to his sides.

The figure was definitely a man and one who was larger in body mass than Henry. Since they were almost the same height, with the attacker being an inch or two taller, Henry threw back his head and hit him in the face, stunning him. The grip around his arms slackened and he freed himself, but before he could fully get away, he was tackled to the ground. The man tried to kick Henry but he rolled out of the way and gained his feet as fast as he could. The attacker then pulled out a knife.

He had to bring this man down and question him. He pulled the gun out of his pocket and aimed it.

"Stand back or I will shoot."

The attacker stopped advancing but Henry still cocked the pistol in readiness to shoot, just in case. "Why have you been following us?" he demanded.

"I am not here to answer stupid questions, detective. I come with a warning. Stop digging for the truth."

With lightning speed, the man threw something at Henry, and in reaction, he pulled the trigger. The attacker clutched his arm and loped off before Henry could do anything more. It was only when he was lowering his arm that he noticed the knife wedged in his shoulder. He began to feel the pain.

He reached to pull it out, but quickly changed his mind. He was already bleeding, but pulling it out could mean more blood and he did not want to risk losing too much blood. Not here.

He swayed on his feet, blinking as his vision began to blur. Moving as quickly as his failing body would allow, he picked up the bag he had been carrying all day with his good arm, and staggered out into the main street.

The further he walked, the weaker his body got and he greatly suspected poisoning. No matter how deep the knife had gone into his shoulder, it was too soon for his body to become this poorly. It felt like a never-ending journey but he reached the house eventually. Libby's house. He used his last strength to lift the brass knocker and on release, his legs gave way and he crashed to the ground.

GRACE, LIBBY'S MAID, WAS ABOUT TO START undoing her corset laces when Anna stormed into the room looking frantic.

"Libby, come quick! It's Detective DeHavillend. He is injured."

Her heart crashed against her rib cage as she dashed for the door. Grace quickly pulled her back and grabbed the dressing gown she had laid out on the bed. Libby speedily covered her body and cinched the sash tightly about her waist before running out with Anna.

Henry was hurt. It was the only thought

running through her head as she ran down the hallway and stairs to the lower level guest room.

He was on the bed lying still, undressed from his waist up, and he did not look like he was breathing. Her hands went up to cover her mouth as her vision blurred with tears. Fear filled her. Antoine and Penforth were standing over him as a footman brought in towels and a pitcher of water.

He was alive! She held the door for balance as relief crashed through her.

Penforth turned and saw her. At first, he waved her away, but must have seen something in her expression as he seemed to change his mind and gestured her to come forward. She did so on shaky legs. There was quite a bit of blood and a knife buried in Henry's right shoulder. The sight made her feel ill.

"W-what...happened?"

"He was stabbed," Pen said grimly. "We suspect he has been poisoned, too."

Libby shut her eyes and looked away. "Has a doctor been called?"

"Yes."

"Who could have done this?" Anna asked.

Libby had an idea. "Someone who doesn't want us searching for the truth," she said, staring at

Henry's still form. Antoine was cleaning the blood around the knife. "Can't the knife be removed?"

"Not yet, my lady. It might make him lose a lot of blood before the doctor arrives."

She buried her face in her hands for a moment and breathed deep. Henry was in this situation because of her. If he—

No, she could not think like that. She *should* not.

"What can I do?" she asked. Pen took her arm to lead her out of the room, but she pulled away. "I need to do something for him, Pen."

"There is nothing you can do right now. There is nothing any of us—save for Antoine—can do at the moment."

"I'll sit with him. I am the reason he is hurt."

"Don't be hard on yourself, Libby." He squeezed her shoulder.

How could she not?

As Pen and Anna left the room, she pulled the chair by the vanity table over to the side of the bed and sat stiffly. Reaching carefully, she took his left hand in both of hers, stroking it gently, and pleading with him to be all right and to forgive her.

Their family doctor, Dr. Poole, arrived half an hour later. One part of her wanted to flee and not watch the doctor work on him, while the other wanted to remain and support him. Libby chose the latter.

She conceded her place beside him and moved to the window while Dr. Poole and Antoine worked together. Antoine had some medical background and treated minor wounds quite well. This was out of his depth because of the suspected poisoning.

With incredible care, Dr. Poole placed his hand on Henry's shoulder so the blade was between his thumb and forefinger then pressed his palm down as he swiftly pulled out the knife. Blood gushed, causing Libby to momentarily lose her composure.

The blood was cleaned away and Dr. Poole stitched the wound neatly.

"I believe he will be all right. We only have to watch for infection," he said, when he was through treating him.

"What about the poisoning?" Libby asked.

"It appears to be some kind of muscle relaxant. Thankfully, the patient has some returning function in his limbs, though I believe he may remain rather sleepy for a day or so. He is breathing on his own, which is a good sign. The effects should resolve completely with time. I suspect the aim was to disable temporarily, rather than kill."

Relief rushed through her. Henry would be fine. Eventually.

Pen showed Dr. Poole out and at Libby's request, everyone left her alone with Henry, although the door remained open for propriety. She took his hand again, determined to remain with him until he woke.

She was certain that this was the work of their stalker. However, she was unsure if Henry was attacked suddenly or if he saw the stalker and followed. It didn't matter which. It would not stop her from investigating. But now she would do so while keeping Henry safe. In this house.

The following morning

"LIBBY," CAME A WHISPER.

She started and raised her head from the bed. Anna was standing beside her with a gentle hand on her shoulder. Had she drifted off to sleep? A look around told her it was morning. One of the powder blue curtains had been opened a touch to allow natural light to filter in.

"You should go upstairs and get some proper sleep. I'll watch him."

She sat up with a sigh. Anna was right. Her body ached all over and she was exhausted. She studied Henry, who had a better color in his face this morning. Where he was barely breathing last night, now his bare chest rose and fell rhythmically.

"Wake me if he wakes up," she said, struggling to her feet.

A moan stopped her procession and she turned in time to see his eyes open. Moving back to the bed, she leaned over him, calling his name. His silvery eyes were unfocused and he stared blankly ahead.

"I don't think he is awake," Anna observed.

No, he was not.

"Go on and get some rest."

Anna would not allow her to stay and she did not have the strength to argue this morning. Pen appeared in the doorway as she was leaving.

"How is he?" her brother asked.

"He seems stable and he opened his eyes just now, but not from wakefulness. I think he is a little improved, though."

Pen nodded. "You should rest, Libby. I'll make sure he's comfortable and looked after."

She agreed and left Henry in their care. She got into bed once she was in her room and the instant her head touched the pillow, she was taken away by slumber.

W<small>HEN SHE WOKE, IT WAS ALREADY MID-AFTERNOON</small> and the first thing she did was inquire about Henry before having a bath and getting dressed.

Nothing had changed. Dr. Poole *had* said the effects of the muscle poison could last up to a day. She tried not to worry, but it was not easy.

When she arrived at his bed chamber, she found her mother seated beside him, reading.

"Mama," she said quietly as she approached.

Christiana looked up and smiled a little. "How are you, Libby?"

Good question. How was she?

"I don't know," she replied, looking at Henry. Beads of sweat covered his forehead and beside Christiana was a bowl filled with water and a towel. "Does he have a fever?"

Her mother nodded. "He did. Dr. Poole called again while you were sleeping. He said to expect the fever to break, which it now has. He will be fine." Christiana marked her page and closed the book in her hand before rising to her feet. "Would you like to sit with him?"

"Yes, please."

On her way out, Christiana paused. "I know

what is going through your mind, Libby. Don't blame yourself. It is not your fault."

Her throat and chest constricted with emotion and she swallowed hard. She might lift the blame off herself when he recovered, or at least when he was awake.

She sat for a long time just watching him, then she grew restless. Sitting still was not her thing and she needed to find something to do. She went to the library to retrieve a book and when she returned, his body was trembling. The fever had returned.

Well, *there* was what she had asked for. Something to occupy her. She pulled the bed covers from his body so as not to encourage the fever to take full hold, although she suspected that it already had. Then she wet a clean towel and began to gently mop his brow.

Two days later

BOTH HENRY'S BODY AND HIS STATE OF MIND TOLD him that he was in trouble and trapped in sleep. He had tried to wake several times and every time he got close, something would pull him back to the bottom and he would have to start all over again.

There had been bouts of intense cold and then intense heat. The cold had been harder to bear because it came with a looped dream. It would be horrible at first, where someone would be throwing knives at him and then it would change and he would find a comfortable bed and lay down, warm and safe.

It was very difficult. He did not know where he was or what was happening to him and he was afraid.

But through the darkness, he felt the presence of people. People who were trying to help him. There was one presence that struck him the most. He enjoyed her voice and her touch. He was more aware now and he could clearly hear her voice. Henry followed it, held on to it to pull him out of this darkness.

His eyelids felt incredibly heavy, like he had not used them in a while and his throat was extremely dry. "Henry," she whispered. "Come back to me."

The soft melody made him smile. He wanted to see her lovely face, but his eyes were not cooperating.

Soft hands touched his brow and then smoothed his hair. It gave him a beautiful, blissful feeling. He relaxed again, not minding very much that he was still unable to open his eyes.

Sleep took him again, but this time he did not get lost and he did not have to fight anything. He was safe, and when he was ready, he followed her voice and her touch once again.

He opened his eyes. The brightness that hit him was a bit overwhelming at first but with slow blinking and patience, his eyes adjusted and he was able to see.

He had thought that her face would be hovering over him, but only a white ceiling greeted him. His hands moved searchingly and they connected with hers.

He sighed with relief. She was there. "Libby," he croaked, wincing at the dryness in his throat and the odd taste in his mouth.

"Welcome back to the world of the living," she said.

He turned his head, and her smile was so brilliant he felt as if he could be in heaven.

"It's so good to see you," he said, smiling back.

She didn't say anything, only clutched more tightly at his hand.

"How long have I been dead?"

She frowned and gave him a warning look. "That is not funny, Henry."

He laughed weakly. "Forgive me. How long have I been asleep?"

"That is much better. About three days."

Good Lord! He had been asleep for three *days*?

The memory came flooding in as he was about to ask what had happened. The stalker had escaped and he had not been able to chase after him because...

"Was I poisoned?"

She nodded solemnly. "Some kind of muscle thing that made you weak and put you to sleep for a while."

Holy God!

"The doctor said the amount was not enough to kill you."

"Hmm. Good thing, that." He closed his eyes briefly, trying to dismiss all thoughts of what might have been.

"I just glad you're all right," she said softly.

"So am I, Libby."

He tried to sit up, but his dearth of strength caused his body to feel weighted and he sighed.

"Give yourself time, Henry. You've only just woken." Libby reached for a cup on the dresser and raised it to his lips. "Boiled and cooled water," she explained. "It will help your throat."

He allowed her to feed him the drink and the coolness of it relieved the dryness in his throat and washed away the bitter taste in his mouth.

"Would you like to eat something?"

"Definitely! But I think I will need a bath first."

Libby's cheeks colored a delightful shade of pink. "Oh, right. I'll get Antoine. He is handy with wounds and Dr. Poole was happy to leave you in his care."

He watched her leave, wondering how long she had sat with him. She looked tired, and he remembered feeling her presence most of the time.

His heart swelled with emotion.

A short while later, Antoine walked in and when he saw Henry, a soft expression touched his features. It was a first in Henry's experience. The man had never cared to give him a look other than that of condescension.

"It is good to see you awake, Sir," he said. A footman followed behind him carrying wound dressing items and a stack of towels.

"Believe me, I'm pretty pleased, too."

The butler smiled then.

How near death had he been exactly, for the Armstrong-Leeds butler to be nice to him?

"I will see to your wound now, Sir," Antoine informed him as he leaned over and began peeling off the bandage covering his wound. "And then we will run you a bath."

After his wound had been redressed and a hot

bath had been run, Henry pulled himself out of the bed and walked carefully to the bath. He was feeling incredibly weak and when first he was vertical, dizziness assailed him. Antoine assisted, and when he lay back in the warm water, sleep threatened to claim him once again.

*L*ibby was waiting in the drawing room for Henry to be through with his bath, when a footman walked in carrying a valise and a letter.

"This was just delivered for you, Lady Elizabeth," he said.

"Who is it from?" she asked with a somewhat puzzled frown. As she held out her hand to collect the missive, Antoine passed by.

"From someone in Lex—"

"Please, excuse me," she cut the footman off and rushed after the butler. "Is Detective DeHavillend through?"

"Yes, my lady. I am going to have his meal sent in now," he replied.

Good.

Libby picked up her heavy velvet skirt and started to head toward Henry's room, but stopped short, feeling like there was something she was forgetting. Turning, she found the footman in the drawing room doorway looking unsure as to what to do with the valise and the letter.

"Can you have those taken up to my rooms, please?"

He bowed and she continued on to Henry's bed chamber. She found him back in bed. She was about to leave him to sleep when he opened his eyes and directed his silver gaze at her.

"Are you going to come in or are you going to lurk there like a thief?"

Libby smiled widely as she stepped into the room and went to the chair by his bed. He was clean-shaven and looked stronger than when he had first woken up.

"How are you?"

"Hungry."

"*That* is a good sign." She wanted to ask him about what had happened that night and discuss an idea she had been considering, but endeavored to restrain herself until he had eaten.

Antoine cleared his throat to announce himself from the hallway. He walked in with a footman carrying a loaded tray that he set down on the bed beside Henry.

"Compliments of Lady Christiana, Sir," Antoine announced.

"Please extend my gratitude."

The food was not the typical food given to a convalescing person, which more often than not would be soup. Her mother made sure Henry had a full three-course meal: soup, roast beef with vegetables and potatoes, and a slice of decadent cake.

"I was not expecting this," he admitted.

"My mother takes our meals very seriously."

"I can see that." He balanced the soup bowl on his lap and started eating.

Libby watched him shamelessly. She surmised he did not eat like this very often. He was a bachelor and his work took a lot of his time. He devoured everything fast until he came to the cake, which he ate very slowly.

"Your sweet tooth at play?" she asked.

"Mmm hmm."

Once he was done, he sighed with some contentment. "Do you know when the doctor is coming back?" he asked.

"This evening, I believe."

"I need to know how soon I can return to work."

There was the opening she had been waiting for.

"Don't you think it's too soon to be thinking of that?"

He placed the empty cake plate back onto the tray and wiped his mouth with a napkin before shaking his head. "There is a killer out there. We need to find him."

"*I* need to find him."

Henry's gaze narrowed suspiciously. "*You* need to find him?"

"Henry, what exactly happened that night?"

"I saw our stalker after I left you. He must have been following us again. I went after him and we scuffled in an alley. He stabbed me but I was able to get a shot in, at least. I got him in the arm."

Libby felt worse than she had earlier now that she had confirmation that he had been wounded because of her.

"I cannot allow you to continue with this case, Henry," she said solemnly, her eyes fixed on her hands on her lap.

"You can't be serious."

She looked at him now. "I mean it, Henry. You went through all of this because of me. I couldn't live with myself if anything more were to happen to you."

Libby cared deeply for Henry. She had acknowledged the extent of her feelings the night of his attack, and although she had come to terms with the reality that she might never be his, she could not bear it if something worse happened to him.

"Nothing is going to happen, Libby. I will be more cautious."

"I've never met anyone more cautious, Henry."

He reached over and took her hand. "I can't do that. I can't live with myself if I don't finish this, just like you can't live with yourself if something happens to me. Please understand, Libby."

"Don't do that," she muttered, emotion thickening her voice. "Do not use my own argument against me."

His lips curved in a sly smile. "It's working, then?"

She pulled her hand from his. "I am not going to talk about this anymore. Once you are well, you will go home and continue to search for Lady Kingsleigh's necklace and forget this case ever existed."

"Now you are being ridiculous."

"What is ridiculous about trying to save you?" Her words were snappier than she intended.

"I don't need to be saved," he snapped back.

"I am quite through with this conversation," she said coolly, before rising and leaving the room.

ELIZABETH'S RESOLUTENESS IN TRYING TO KEEP HIM off the case was flattering but she would not win against him. Starting this had been a choice, but finishing it had become a responsibility to Henry.

She had no say in that anymore, especially now that he was acquainted with her family. They were decent people and they did not deserve this misfortune.

He wanted to call her back, but she was a woman who felt things strongly. Allowing her a moment to regain her bearing was necessary if he wanted to convince her to let him finish solving the case.

With a weary sigh, Henry leaned back against the pillows and closed his eyes. Damn poison. It had really taken his energy.

"Henry," came Mary's voice.

He turned his head to see her in the doorway. As usual, the brown cat Treacle was with her.

"How are you feeling?" she asked, stepping into the room.

"I am much better, thank you Mary."

"You gave us quite the scare, especially Libby."

Knowing that Libby cared about him enough to be worried when he was unwell was rather comforting.

"My apologies."

She laughed. "Oh, don't apologize, silly. It was beyond your control. Besides, we are all happy you're recuperating in our home and not alone." She sat in the chair Libby had vacated.

Henry wondered what would have happened if he had gone to his apartments instead. He would have had it worse because there would have been no one to take care of him, not even to call him a doctor and stitch him up.

Suddenly, his solitary life did not hold as much appeal as it did before.

"I should ring for someone to take that tray away," Mary said. He was grateful to her for rescuing him from his thoughts.

When she rose, Treacle jumped onto the bed, landing on Henry's lap. It kneaded his quilt for a moment, seeking the most comfortable spot.

"He likes you," Mary declared.

"I can see that," he murmured, surprised.

Having the cat sleep on his lap gave him a cozy feeling. He reached out and stroked the soft fur. It began to purr and Mary laughed.

"The two of you are going to get along just fine," she said, then turned serious. "Henry, I wanted to ask if you need any help with the case while you are recovering. Look for clues, perhaps."

How thoughtful of her, but he needed to protect not only Libby but her family.

"Thank you for the offer but you should stay home with your family where you are safe. I will finish the case when I am better."

She nodded. "I understand. Would you like me to help with Lady Kingsleigh's case then?"

That was not a bad idea. Far less dangerous than stalkers and murderers.

"I had a bag with me when I came. Do you kno—"

"That bag?" she asked, pointing at a brown leather bag in the corner.

"Yes."

"I knew the bag was important so I had them place it there after cleaning."

"Cleaning?"

"Only the outside. It was dirty. I was there when it was done so nothing inside got tampered with."

He smiled in relief. "Thank you. Can you bring the bag here, please?"

Since she had pushed her way into being his apprentice, they might as well discuss the Kingsleigh case. He was stuck—more out of disinterest—and a different mind might view it from a different angle and perhaps find something he had missed.

She retrieved the bag and brought it to the bed, then opened it at his directive, pulling out the Kingsleigh folder.

"Everything about the case is there. You may study it and we can discuss it later. But my condition still holds. You cannot be my apprentice unless you obtain your brother and mother's permission."

Her eyes gleamed with excitement. "Of course. Oh, my first case! I will do my best."

He nodded, feeling his eyelids grow heavy.

"I'll let you sleep," she said just as a footman entered to retrieve his food tray.

She closed the door behind her and everything went quiet save for Treacle's soft purrs and the fire crackling in the fireplace.

This was very comfortable, indeed.

WHEN LIBBY RETURNED TO HER ROOM, UPSET WITH Henry but even more upset with herself, she sat on the bed unsure what to do. He was a very stubborn man, but then so was she. In a way, they complemented each other.

She felt a smile softening her frown as tenderness replaced her ire. They were both crazy, Henry, and herself. They were both trying to protect each other.

A brown valise sitting near her vanity table caught her attention, reminding her of the unexpected delivery that afternoon.

Libby walked over to it and found the letter resting on top. There was an address on the envelope: *The Blue Chapel*, Lexington.

Her heart skipped a beat when she saw the address. It was where she'd been forced to marry her captor, and where she had been locked in the crypt for a long time.

Squeezing her eyes shut, she prayed for fortitude; the courage to face whatever was in that letter and the valise, for it could not be anything good.

With trembling fingers, she tore open the envelope and pulled out the letter, her heart resounding in her ears:

Dear Baroness Esk,

I pray this message finds you well. Allow me a moment to introduce myself. I am Joseph Roth, the new warden of The Blue Chapel.

Upon my assumption of the post, I found the belongings of the late Mr. Nolan Hart. Since the church records prove that you are his wife, I have forwarded his belongings to you.

My deepest condolences and may his soul find peace.
Sincerely,
Mr. Joseph Roth

Libby blinked several times. The church warden believed that she was Mr. Hart's wife and had sent his belongings to her. Did he not know that she had been kidnapped by this man after he had written several letters posing as a gentleman? If he had received news of Nolan Hart's death, then surely, he must have known of the man's misdoings.

Nevertheless, the belongings were here and she would have to check them.

An idea formed and glowed in her mind, chasing away her dread. Who knew what clues she could find in that valise?

She knelt beside the bag and quickly undid the buckles.

All she could see, at first, were items of clothing,

but as she removed them, she found a journal, marriage papers—papers with which he'd hoped to get his hands on her fortune—and a stack of letters. *Her* letters.

The letters she had written with a smile on her face and a dream in her heart. Her chest tightened and her throat constricted as she removed them from the bottom of the bag. They were stacked and tied together by a string of leather.

Part of her wanted to open them and read, remind herself of the folly that had gotten her into this mire; another part wanted to throw them into the fire and forget they ever existed.

But the truth was that she would never forget. The flames would not burn away her pain and embarrassment.

Libby rose with the stack of letters in her hand and approached the fire. Taking a deep breath, she threw them in and watched the fire flare up, engulfing them.

As she had expected, burning the letters did not burn away her mistakes nor make her feel any better.

She returned to the man's belongings and picked up the journal. As she flipped the pages, a key slid out from one of the pages and landed on the carpet.

Libby picked it up to examine: It looked very similar to the key Pen held for the family's bank lockbox. Was this another lockbox key? If so, where was the box?

Carefully, she lowered herself onto the bed and began going through the journal properly. She wasn't sure what she was looking for, but didn't want to miss anything.

Several pages in, she saw her name and her address, but that was it. She continued reading. He had been a well-traveled man according to the journal. Some of what he'd said in his letters might have been true.

Farther in, she found a bank name and an address. She looked from the key in her hand to the contents of the page. Was this the key to a lockbox in that bank?

Her heart pounded with nervous excitement as she continued to search through the journal for clues, but she came up empty. Perhaps the thing to do was go to the bank and try to open the box. But she couldn't do that by herself. She would need Henry's help so he could act as both witness and as detective on the case should they find something serious.

She could never have kept him off the case anyway. She knew that already.

Taking the key and the journal with her, she went to Henry's room. When she opened the door, he was sound asleep with Treacle beside him, also sleeping. The sight tugged at her inmost sentiments.

When one saw Henry for the first time, you would never imagine he might be caught sleeping with an adorable cat curled up alongside him. It spoke of his innate gentleness; those layers beneath that he clearly did not wish others to know about. But now, Libby knew. And she liked what she had seen.

She gently closed the door and went back to her room.

When he woke, they would decide what to do next. Together.

The following day

HENRY FELT MUCH IMPROVED THE NEXT MORNING. He had regained enough of his strength to walk without easily becoming fatigued, but the family insisted he not move back to his apartments just yet.

He had to admit, it was nice to feel cared for.

The first thing he did was send a message to

Montgomery informing him of what had happened and his condition.

An hour later, Antoine informed him that the District Commander was here to see him. Henry was astonished. That was quick. Most of the household was still abed.

Instead of having Montgomery see him bleary-eyed and in a robe, he got dressed—in borrowed clothes from Penforth—and made his way to the salon.

"Glad to see you're on your feet," Montgomery said, on seeing him. "You look very out of sorts though."

Henry mustered a smile. "Can you blame me?"

"Hardly."

Henry sat down. He was not well enough to stand for long. "I know you didn't come here to check on me, Sir. So, what can I do for you?"

"I am here for a statement from you. Your attacker needs to be found."

Henry chuckled darkly. "Have you all finally decided to do the right thing?"

A protracted silence followed his question before Montgomery finally answered. "I have thought a lot about what you said. I realize now that we cannot pick and choose which cases to solve and which not to in order to satisfy the elite. It is not right."

Well, that appeared to be the start of something good. A reformation.

"I am happy to hear that."

"We are starting with this case. We need to finish it and in order to do that, I will need that report from you."

Henry described the hooded man who had attacked him, then had his bag brought so he could give Montgomery the strands of hair and the sample of perfumed grease he'd found.

"I think that might be a pomade of some kind. It was on the brick in the alleyway in Roxbury, together with the hair and blood, and it certainly has a very distinctive odor. It smells like a match for what Burris described he had found on the deceased man's head, but I will leave it to him to confirm that."

"I will send some officers to Roxbury immediately." Montgomery's tone changed then, and his voice softened. "You will stay out of trouble while we get that done?"

"I may love danger and adventure, Commander, but I have only one body."

The commander rose to his feet. "Take care, Henry."

He remained seated in the salon for some time, thinking. He was greatly pleased with

Montgomery's change of heart and the effort he was going put into reforming the police.

A knock sounded on the door and he turned to find Sir Penforth standing in the doorway. He must have known about Montgomery's call.

"Good morning, Penforth," he greeted. The two were now on first name terms.

"I am glad to see you are doing better, Henry." He walked into the room and took a seat adjacent to Henry.

"That was Commander Montgomery," Henry supplied.

"Yes, I gathered."

"He has had a change of heart and is willing to see this case to a proper conclusion. So, he came for a report himself."

"That change is thanks to you, I'll bet." Penforth smiled a little then, and in the depths of his eyes, Henry caught something quite like respect. "I never got the chance to thank you for helping Libby. For believing in her."

"You don't have to."

"I think I do. Libby is my sister."

Henry smiled. "Says the man who rescued her himself when the police did nothing."

Penforth smiled more widely this time. "That credit goes to my fiancée, Anna."

"In that case, Libby should have the credit for this. She has found all the leads thus far."

Penforth nodded. "Breakfast?"

"Please."

Without further ceremony, the two men went to the dining room for a companionable breakfast, while the ladies were just waking up.

CHAPTER SIXTEEN

*T*he trophy room was the last place she had expected to find Henry. Deep voices echoed through the quiet hallway of the first floor and when she arrived, Pen was showing Henry some of the oldest in his collection of firearms.

When Penforth and Anna had rescued her and brought her home, they had met a mob outside their home: gossipy aristocrats, curious passersby, and vulture-like reporters. Entry into the house for Libby and the others had been nearly impossible. A couple of their footmen had retrieved firearms from this room on Antoine's direction and intimidated the mob to clear a path.

Prior to her abduction, she had not cared for the collection one way or another, but after that event, she had been glad they were here in the house.

Libby knocked gently on the door to gain their attention.

The men turned at the same time and she smiled at them. Henry grinned back, causing a flutter to rise in her stomach.

"Which one of us are you looking for?" Pen asked.

"Sorry, Pen, it's Henry," she replied jokingly.

"Are you not going to come in?" Henry asked, after Pen had left.

She realized that she was still standing in the doorway and blushed a little. She stepped into the room.

"How are you?" They asked the question in unison, then burst out laughing.

"You first," he offered.

"I am quite well."

"And I am feeling much better." He opened his arms to show her how well he looked. "As you can see."

His improvement gladdened and relieved her.

"Do you want to sit? There is something I want to talk to you about."

His expression turned serious and he directed them to a small sitting area in a corner of the room. It was a cozy-looking place with a patterned rug, a chair, and a couch upholstered in chocolate brown velvet. Honestly, they always reminded her of chocolate. He took the chair while she sat on the sofa, placing Mr. Hart's journal beside her.

Then she removed the key from her dress pocket and placed it on the journal. "I received an unexpected package yesterday afternoon. It's from the new warden of *The Blue Chapel*."

Immediately the place was mentioned, Henry's features darkened.

"Is that not the—"

"Yes, it is. The minister sent Mr. Hart's belongings to me because he believes I am his wife."

"Doesn't he know what happened?" Henry's voice rose. "You were abducted. The marriage is not real."

"It is real, Henry," she said in a small voice. "But that aside, I thought the same thing when I read his letter."

Henry anger on her behalf was rather endearing.

"I found something of note, however." She picked up the journal and the key and proffered them to him. "I believe this is a bank lockbox key. The journal doesn't contain any pertinent information besides the address of the bank where I assume the lockbox is kept."

He collected the items and examined them carefully. When he finished, he said, "What are you thinking? Check it out?"

"Yes, I think so. Perhaps we will find something that might help solve the case at last."

"A bank lockbox?" There was a strange tone in his voice and Libby's guard immediately went up. Was she being condescended to?

"It could contain anything," she countered. "We should check."

"In my experience, they almost always contain jewelry, financial papers or a will, but never murder clues. In many cases they are empty."

"Maybe this will be a first. I have a strong feeling about it."

He shook his head. "I think your strong feeling is misplaced." He dropped the items onto a black lacquered side table.

"Henry, you can't just dismiss this as irrelevant."

His silver gaze held hers and he leaned forward slightly. "I think you should leave this line of inquiry alone, Libby."

His words, or more specifically, his obvious lack of trust in her instincts, hurt. She had thought that they understood and trusted each other.

Tears began to well up in her eyes. "I really thought you were willing to help me."

"Of course, I am willing to help you."

"Clearly not." With that, she picked up the journal and the key and stalked out of the room.

If he wouldn't help her, she would do it herself. She had started this investigation alone, and that's how she'd finish it. It was wrong to have relaxed her guard and she would no longer hold him to promises that were obviously empty.

The following day

As early as nine o'clock, Libby was out of the house and on her way to the bank to retrieve whatever was in that box. She was not wearing that dreadful disguise. She did not need to hide anymore.

When she had woken, resolve filled her. No one would stop her finding out the truth. She snuck out the way she had always done and walked down the street to find a hire carriage.

Predictably, she was being followed. However, she was not as afraid as she had been previously. Her resolve and anger—with Henry, with her circumstances, and with the murderer--carried her along regardless.

The bank mentioned in the journal was in Roxbury. Why did it have to be *there*? She sighed. The last couple of days had been very difficult and she was feeling the toll, but she plowed on. What other choice did she have?

The bank turned out to be a rather small and obscure place, with only three employees inside. She approached the man closest and identified herself.

He simpered when he learned who she was, no doubt wondering if her family would bring some business to their establishment.

"I need to access my late husband's deposit box," she said without preamble. "Can you help me with that?"

"Of course, my lady. May I have his name and proof of the marriage?"

She presented the marriage papers she'd found in Mr. Hart's belongings; glad they were included in his things.

"Yes, that is one of ours." Her heart leapt. She had found it! "Please follow me, my lady."

Libby followed him into a room with floor to ceiling safe boxes on one wall, and a table with a couple of chairs positioned on the other side of the room.

"Your husband's box is number sixty-two." He pointed at the box with the number. "I'll leave you to it."

Once he was out of the room with the door closed firmly behind him, Libby inserted the key into the lock and when it turned, she took a deep breath.

She had no idea what she would find, and whether or not it would be relevant, but she was hopeful. She had to trust her own instincts. Especially now that Henry had disregarded them.

The box contained a black velvet case and Libby reached in and pulled it out. It was a triangular necklace case. Carrying it to the table, she opened it slowly, revealing an expensive-looking necklace featuring a huge ruby in the center, sitting in velvet luxury.

Nolan Hart could never have afforded to buy such a brilliant piece. It must be stolen goods.

How would this help her case, though?

She didn't want to consider that Henry might have been right. And she certainly was not going to share the information with him. In fact, she decided, he was off the case, and once he was well enough to leave their house, she would ensure he returned to his own life and she would never have to endure seeing him again.

Think about all of that when I get home. She closed the jewelry case and then relocked the box before stepping out of the room.

The banker rose from his desk. "I trust you have found what you are looking for, my lady?"

She nodded. "Yes, I have. Thank you for your assistance."

"We hope to see you again soon." He bowed.

She inclined her head regally before stepping out of the bank and onto the street with the jewelry case clutched under her arm. There was no other way to carry it, since she had only a small reticule with her.

As she walked, a feeling of urgency increased. Where was her stalker? She almost wanted the person to materialize, so she could confront them at last. She turned her head, scanning her surroundings, and saw nothing until she reached an alleyway. A flash of movement out of the corner of her eye was all the warning she had, before she was suddenly dragged to the side and thrown onto the ground.

HENRY COULDN'T BELIEVE SHE HAD BEATEN HIM here. How early had she risen? He'd had every intention of following up on the new clue at the bank, especially when he recognized the insignia on the key as a location in Roxbury, but had hoped to keep Libby safe for once, from exactly this situation.

His heart felt as if it stopped in his chest when he saw someone pull her roughly into the alleyway. His blood rushed to his legs to propel him forward. His shoulder pained him as he moved but he put that out of his head. Shoulder pain was the least of his worries.

Libby had gotten herself into trouble again, and she was more important to him than anything.

He raced into the alley to find another woman on top of Libby struggling with her. He ran forward to separate them and found that they were scuffling over a black velvet box.

Henry dragged the woman off Libby and she fell to the ground, then he quickly knelt and pinned her down before she could recover and attack again. A bruise was starting to color on her cheek. Libby had clearly gotten in a most unladylike punch. Good for her!

But the woman was holding the box.

"Who the devil are *you*?" he demanded.

The woman glowered up at him, as Libby bent down and snatched the box back.

She refused to answer and continued to

struggle, though, even in his weakened state, she was no match for his strength.

"Who are you and what do you want?" he asked again.

Libby handed him a long satin ribbon from her cloak, and he bound the woman's hands together before pulling her up to her feet. He still did not let her go.

Finally, the woman spoke. "I am Nolan Hart's *real* wife!"

Libby's jaw dropped, as did his own. "What?"

"I married him last year and he destroyed my life," she cried. "I thought he was a good man and I fell in love. Once we were married, he took all of my inheritance and squandered it. He ruined me. I *had* to do it. I *had* to kill him."

Henry's gaze travelled to Libby as the woman revealed the truth. Libby's face was already pale and her eyes were wide with shock.

"*You* killed Mr. Hart?" Henry asked, just to confirm he had heard correctly the first time.

"Yes, and I don't regret it," the woman spat. "He was a monster. Look what he did to *you*," she said, directly to Libby. "I did us both a favor."

"You tried to *frame* her!" Henry said, and the woman's gaze slid away.

"Well, when I realized that might not work, I decided to…" She trailed off.

"You decided to spread the rumor about the Raven?" Henry prompted.

"Someone had to take the blame."

"So, you know the man who attacked me."

"Yes, I hired him to slow your investigation."

"Where is he now?"

She shrugged. "I don't know. I never saw him again after you wounded him. He has not even collected his last payment."

"What do you want with the ruby necklace?" Libby finally spoke.

Necklace? Henry shifted his gaze to the velvet box.

"It belonged to my grandmother," the woman sniffed. "It's the only valuable thing I have left and I have been searching for it. It is why I have been following you. I thought you might eventually lead me to it."

Henry wasn't quite sure he fully believed her. Being ruined and left penniless was a terrible fate, but it was still no reason to commit murder. Nor to frame an innocent person for a crime they did not commit.

"I just want my grandmother's necklace back,

please." The woman began to sob, but he noticed she didn't have any tears.

While he was debating within himself, Libby loosened the ribbon binding the woman's hands.

"Wait," he started to say, but it was too late. She had handed the velvet box back to the woman.

"I just wish you hadn't actually killed him," Libby said with a sigh.

"He was a monster!" the woman exclaimed again.

Libby shook her head. "It's still no reason to kill someone. Take your necklace."

"Enjoy your freedom while it lasts, because the police *will* come after you," Henry warned her. "I'll make sure of it."

She ran out of the alley. When Henry turned to Libby, her eyes were filled with tears. "I had to let her go," she said. "That woman's fate could have been mine."

She shuddered, and without thinking, he pulled her into his arms. "Never," he said. "You would never have taken the actions that *criminal* took. But it's over now," he said in a low soothing voice. "We know who did it. And, if she married Mr. Hart last year, why, there should be no opposition to your own annulment. It's good news, Libby."

She sniffed before pulling away. "What are you

doing here? I thought you had stopped believing in me."

He tightened his hold briefly before releasing her. "Of course, I believed you. And in you. I just wanted to protect you, for once."

"You were wrong."

"Yes, I was," he admitted. "I should have honored our commitment to work together. I am so sorry, Libby. Will you forgive me?"

"I don't want to talk now, Henry. I just want to go home." She began walking out of the alley and he had no choice but to follow.

She was still upset with him. And why should she not be? He had paid lip service to the two of them being equal partners in this, and then by his actions, had done the opposite. The fact that his motivation was purely to protect someone he cared about, was moot.

He was in the wrong.

His carriage was waiting at the end of the road and when he offered to hand her in, she ignored him and climbed up by herself.

The ride to her home was made in silence with enough tension to suck the life out of him, but he remained patient.

He cared about Libby, and now that the case was over—well, almost over—he would do whatever he could to make amends. She had become too precious to let go.

When they reached Armstrong-Leeds House, she left him and headed straight upstairs to her own suite. He sat in the drawing room feeling out of place and somewhat drained. He supposed he did not have to stay here anymore. He had almost recovered completely, and the case was all but concluded.

"What happened?" Penforth's voice washed over him and he stirred.

"We found the killer," he said simply. "It was a woman. Mr. Nolan Hart's real wife."

Penforth's eyes widened and he strode into the room. What on earth?" He rubbed his chin. "So, Libby's marriage to the man, forced or otherwise, is null and void."

Henry nodded. "That is correct."

"Thank God!" Penforth ran his hands through his hair. His relief was palpable.

"Libby received some of Mr. Hart's belongings from the chapel two days ago and there was a key to a bank deposit box in the items. It turned out to contain a ruby necklace that the wife had been looking for. She has been following us for days, hoping we'll lead her to it. We tussled with her before she revealed that he married her last year and conned her out of her inheritance. In order to enact revenge, she killed him. The necklace was her grandmother's so Libby gave it back to her."

"You let the woman go?" Pen asked.

"Just for now. I will ensure the police go after her. Libby has a soft heart and she believed everything the woman said. I'm not so sure. And I damn well will *not* allow a murderer to get away with it, not after all she put Libby through," he avowed.

"Thank you, Detective, for everything you have done for our family."

Henry gave him a slow nod.

"Are you certain you don't want payment?"

He started to shake his head but stopped. "Actually, I do have a request."

CHAPTER SEVENTEEN

*L*ibby was not sure how long she sat on her bed thinking, but she was beyond relieved. The nightmare that had seemed never-ending was now over. Once the truth was revealed, and her annulment complete, she could go out into the world again, face people, and Mary could make her debut and not be ruined.

But her heart ached. Of course, she was still annoyed with Henry, but she knew deep down that his motivation had been true. He must care for her, at least a little, and had only wished to protect her. Perhaps he just needed more instruction in the ways of equality for all. Or perhaps, now that the case was ended, he would disappear out of her life forever. Not long ago she had wished for that. Now she couldn't imagine anything worse.

The door opened suddenly and Anna rushed in, jumped onto the bed, and took Libby in her arms. "Pen just gave me wonderful news!"

Libby grinned. "I am free, Anna, or at least, I will be soon, and so is Mary."

Anna's blue eyes shimmered. "We are going to give her the biggest ball to celebrate her entrance into society."

"I agree."

"Libby!" Mary ran in and jumped onto the bed too, hugging both Libby and Anna. "I am so happy this is over!"

It was truly a beautiful moment and Libby could not be more grateful for her beautiful family and friends. She was safe, and once they reported to the police, her name would be cleared. It was wonderful.

But was she truly happy?

Christiana joined them then. "I am so proud of you, Libby. You went out and found the truth. You remind me a lot of your father. He never wavered in the face of adversity. I was always the one crying and being afraid."

Libby wrapped her arms around her mother. "I love you, Mama."

"I love you too, my dear brave child."

They became quiet, appreciating the moment

and their blessings, until Mary broke the silence with an announcement.

"I have solved the stolen necklace case."

Stolen necklace? Libby was confused because she had just finished dealing with a necklace. But then realization came and she laughed. "Lady Kingsleigh's necklace?"

"Henry put me on the case. I know who did it. It was her lady's maid." Mary's dark eyes gleamed with excitement and adventure. "He had collected all the clues, you see; names and portraits. I noticed that the lady's maid looked suspiciously familiar, and on closer inspection, I discovered that it is the same maid caught searching Libby's room. Do you remember her?"

They all nodded, and Mary continued. "In the police statement, she said she is French, but we know that is a lie. She was born right here in Boston. She just changed her accent."

Christiana blinked. "How did you find out all of this?"

Mary beamed. "I love searching for clues. I have been trying to figure out why she was searching Libby's room. Libby attended a ball the night before and she wore your emerald necklace. I think she was looking for that necklace."

"I am sure, with Henry's guidance, you will do a

wonderful job in solving the mysteries plaguing this city," Christiana said.

Libby believed that, too. Her sister was very intelligent and she had the passion for it. She had just solved a case for which Henry had been too occupied to give his full attention.

"Know that I will not allow you to abandon your life here as Henry has done," her mother cautioned Mary.

The young girl laughed. "Of course not, Mama!"

"Come, we are going to have a feast tonight to celebrate," Christiana said, getting to her feet. "Anna, Mary, come help me prepare. And Libby, I want you to get some rest."

Libby smiled at her mother, looking forward to the celebration. It was long overdue.

Instead of resting as her mother had recommended, Libby left the room to search for Henry. Even though she was still out of sorts about him, she felt the need to see him. She did not even know what she was going to say when she saw him.

On reaching his guest room, she found the space devoid of his presence. All of his things were gone. A maid with an armful of linens was about to attack the bed.

The maid might not know, but Libby asked anyway. "Have you seen the detective?"

The girl bobbed a quick curtsey. "He left just a moment ago."

He left moments ago. He had not even stopped to say goodbye...

Libby leaned against the door jamb, feeling the sting of his actions and regretting her own. She truly cared for Henry; had even dreamed of something beautiful happening between them despite all signs of that being unlikely.

Pain squeezed at her insides. She might have her life back, but now that she'd had a glimpse of new possibilities, the old life didn't seem quite so shiny.

Later that afternoon

"Do you think we should send out last-minute invitations to our neighbors?" Christiana asked.

Libby shook her head immediately. "No, Mama. This should be just family."

They were in the drawing room and her mother was finalizing the dinner plans. Christiana clapped her hands together. "Oh, but I think it is a good idea for society to learn that you are not guilty."

"They will find out soon enough. I am not ready to receive guests just yet."

"Oh. All right," her mother yielded.

"Did you invite Henry, Mama?" Mary asked.

"Of course, I did. Henry is practically family."

Libby winced. "I wish you wouldn't say that."

"Why ever not?"

He left without a word, she wanted to answer, but decided against it. She would only sound petty and foolish. And she did not want anyone knowing how much he affected her.

Christiana suddenly beamed, looking past Libby. "And here he is!"

Libby's heart did a strange flutter. She turned and there he was, dressed in the clothing of a gentleman for the first time since they'd met. He looked quite dashing. He advanced into the room and presented the bouquet of flowers he held to her mother.

"There is nothing I can give you to properly thank you for your hospitality over the past few days, my lady."

"Oh, you needn't address me so formally. Call me Christiana. I consider you family now."

Libby's brows knit together and she did not try to hide her disapproval of the comment.

"The sentiment is mutual," he returned, before turning to Libby. "May I speak with you for a moment, please?"

She gave him a dubious look before rising to her feet with her shoulders straight. She led him to the second drawing room, with strange butterfly sensations making themselves felt in her stomach.

"Libby, I apologize about the lockbox," he said without wasting any time. "I was wrong to hide anything from you. I was wrong to doubt how well we work together, as equal partners. I hurt you, and I regret it immensely."

"Are you saying that because it led to the killer being found?"

He shook his head and raised his silvery eyes to hers. She loved their unusual color. She found herself softening again, opening her heart to those feelings she knew would doom her.

"Forgive me," he murmured, taking her hand.

She kept her hand in his, despite knowing that nothing could ever come of her infatuation with him. Marriage was not for the likes of her. Despite the annulment, her reputation was never going to be pristine enough for Boston society. "The truth is, I already have forgiven you."

Henry suddenly seemed awkward, and his cheeks flushed a faint pink color. "Marry me," he blurted out.

Libby's mouth dropped open. After a few seconds of silence, she managed to close it. "Err…" Her brain swirled as shock coursed through her system. "I beg your pardon?"

His eyes bored into her. "You heard me. Marry me. We can save your reputation if we marry, and I can prove to you—and everyone—that I have your best interests at heart."

"Oh." Just like that, her hopes were dashed. He was proposing marriage to save her reputation and although that was a good thing and it showed his remorse and willingness to make amends, it was not love. "I can't marry you."

She moved toward one of the French windows that looked out onto the pretty rear garden. One of the gardeners had already covered the rose bushes to protect them from the coming winter. Libby wished someone would cover her heart and protect it from hurt. She felt rather than saw Henry come up behind her.

"Why won't you marry me?"

"Because having someone's best interests at heart is not a reason for marriage." She turned to face him. "We are not compatible and I don't see how people like us can make a marriage work."

Something like anger flared in his eyes. Good. Because she was angry too. With him and with herself, and most especially, with this whole situation.

He took hold of her shoulders. "That's not true. We have what it takes to make a marriage work."

"What do we have?" she seethed. "Daily arguing? Because we do seem to be very good at that."

"No. We have *this*..." One of his hands left her shoulder and circled her waist.

Her heart jumped in her chest as he dragged her against him. Before she had any time to process what was happening, his lips descended on hers.

Henry's kiss was not gentle but it awakened her fully to what existed between them. There was passion, and while that did not equate to love, perhaps passion could be tended and turn to love with time.

His lips softened then, becoming persuasive rather than hard. She stopped resisting, enjoying the kiss, and clutched his broad shoulders for support, not trusting her legs to keep her upright.

"Libby," he whispered eventually against her mouth.

"Yes?"

He trailed soft kisses from the corner of her mouth to her jaw and up to the delicate spot just below her ear.

"You feel this, surely?"

"Yes," she admitted. She could feel it, everywhere, in her body and deep in her heart.

"We do have what it takes to have a good marriage." Pulling away, he cradled her face in his large hands and placed another soft kiss on her lips. "Do you believe me?"

She nodded, unable to speak.

He kissed her again only this time, he was so tender her heart ached from it. When he pulled away, she saw what his heart held—a promise. "I don't just want to marry you to save your reputation, Elizabeth."

Libby closed her eyes, loving the sound of her full name on his tongue.

"I have come to care deeply for you. Call me a mad man, but I have fallen in love with you."

Her eyes flew open. "A mad man?"

He grinned. "I must be mad, to want to spend the rest of my life with you. Don't you think?"

"*Oh!*" She punched him on the arm and then gasped when he grunted. "Oh, my goodness. Your injury! I forgot!"

"See what I mean?" He was still grinning. "A mad man, for sure!"

This time, she tentatively returned his smile, rubbing his arm where previously she had punched it.

"I love you, Libby, with all my heart." Henry's voice was low and thick with emotion. "I even spoke to Pen earlier. Obtained his permission. Which, I must say, was given only on the proviso that it was what *you* wanted. It is what you want. Isn't it?"

Her heart felt as if it would break, only this time, with happiness. "Oh, Henry..."

Before she could finish, he lowered himself onto one knee and reached into his jacket pocket before producing a small, green velvet box. When he flipped it open, her breath left her body. The ring sitting proudly in the box was none other than the one they had selected at Mr. Kent's jewelry store back in Roxbury.

It was more beautiful even than the image in the catalog, with the smoky topaz and emerald stones catching the light and reflecting it brilliantly. Libby was awestruck.

"Henry, how did you..."

"When we selected the ring, I truly wanted you to have it, but I had not realized how to give it to you back then. I traveled to Roxbury and retrieved it this afternoon."

Tears filled her eyes and started to blur her vision. She closed them briefly to squeeze them out so she could see his face more clearly. He was magnificent, and she loved him.

"Will you marry me, Your Royal Highness, Princess Elizabeth Armstrong-Leeds, Baroness Esk?"

She held out her left hand. "Yes, Viscount Detective Henry DeHavillend. I believe I will."

Slipping the ring onto her finger, he raised her hand to his lips and kissed her knuckles before rising to his feet and pulling her into his arms.

"I love you," she said and he grinned.

"Just as well," he answered, and bent his head to hers, until a dreamy sigh interrupted them. They both turned toward the door to find three female faces spying on them. When the ladies of the house saw that they had been caught, they rushed into the room, flooding the newly engaged couple with felicitations.

THE FOLLOWING DAY, HENRY INFORMED THE police of his and Libby's findings, and his dearly beloved fiancée's name was cleared at last. And since news traveled faster than trains in this town, society soon learned of both her innocence and her engagement to Viscount DeHavillend. Because there was proof that Nolan Hart had been married to another woman when he kidnapped Libby, the case to annul her marriage was passed without challenge, and Henry was able to obtain a license for their nuptials.

Naturally, everyone who was anyone in Boston society coveted an invitation to their wedding. Mary now could be presented to society when the time was right. All was well in their world.

EPILOGUE

THE BARBICAN

*W*hile the police were conducting their search for Mrs. Nolan Hart, Tamworth Arbusson—known in his own circles as the Raven—had instigated a search of his own. Even in death, a debt must be paid. Nolan Hart had owed him a tremendous amount, an amount that could not be forgiven nor forgotten.

The Raven did not want money. He did not need it. As the bastard son of a duke, Tam may not have had legitimacy, but he still had more money than he knew what to do with. His father's guilt had been assuaged with money, and his own string of clubs was very profitable indeed. What he was after was far more precious; the ruby necklace in the murderer's possession. He did not care what sentimental value it held for her; *his* claim was far greater than hers.

And he would do whatever it took to make it his.

This was not over. Not by a long shot.

The End

Lady Sarah and the Raven's story continues in *Not Quite a Lady*
The Boston Heiresses (Book 3)

Want to go back to where it all began? Read Anna and Pen's story in *Not Quite a Duchess*
The Boston Heiresses (Book 1)

ABOUT THE AUTHOR

Ava Rose writes sweet and clean Victorian historical romance and gothic mystery. Her heroines are feisty and independent and her heroes brooding and swoon-worthy. When she's not writing, Ava looks after the family, pampers various cats, and tries to find a smidgen of time for her husband. She lives in Melbourne, Australia.